THE GILDED CAGE

THE SCIENCE OFFICER: VOLUME 3

BLAZE WARD

The Gilded Cage
Volume 3
Blaze Ward
Copyright © 2015 Blaze Ward
All rights reserved
Published by Knotted Road Press
www.KnottedRoadPress.com

ISBN: 978-1-943663-04-0

Cover art:
Copyright © Innovari | Orbital Space Station And Spaceship Photo

Cover and interior design copyright © 2015 Knotted Road Press

Never miss a release!
If you'd like to be notified of new releases, sign up for my newsletter.

I only send out newsletters once a quarter, will never spam you, or use your email for nefarious purposes. You can also unsubscribe at any time.

http://www.blazeward.com/newsletter/

ALSO BY BLAZE WARD

The Jessica Keller Chronicles

Auberon

Queen of the Pirates

Last of the Immortals

Goddess of War

Flight of the Blackbird

St. Legier

Winterhome

CS-405

Queen Anne's Revenge

Packmule

Persephone

Additional Alexandria Station Stories

The Story Road

Siren

Two Bottles of Wine with a War God

The Science Officer Series:

The Science Officer

The Mind Field

The Gilded Cage

The Pleasure Dome

The Doomsday Vault

The Last Flagship

The Hammerfield Gambit

The Hammerfield Payoff

Doyle Iwakuma Stories

The Librarian

Demigod

Greater Than The Gods Intended

Other Science Fiction Stories

Mymirdons

Moonshot

Menelaus

Earthquake Gun

Moscow Gold

Fairchild

White Crane

***The Collective* Universe**

The Shipwrecked Mermaid

Imposters

AUTHOR NOTE

Life sometimes happens. It intrudes. I had always intended to quickly follow up The Mind Field with this book. I just never planned for it to take me nearly a year to get there.

Wilhelmina Teague returns for the adventure she didn't get to have before. Javier and Suvi get to grow into larger and more interesting characters. The universe, the sandbox, gets richer.

In between then and now, you have the first three Jessica Keller novels: Auberon, Queen of the Pirates, Last of the Immortals. The last one does not bookend this universe. I have other adventures planned for Suvi in Jessica's future, but Jessica is six thousand years in Javier's future.

We are just starting out here, and there is a lot of ground to cover.

There is never enough time to write all the stories I would churn out if I could. On the drive home tonight, as I was climbing the pass, Javier tapped me on the shoulder and explained some of the key bits of what will become his fourth story, after I finish the current project (or projects).

I like writing these as novellas instead of novels. Not because Javier doesn't deserve a novel, but because I can write more of them if I don't have to tell a grand story. Or as grand a story. This is book three, but it is not a trilogy, except in the counting at present. Like I said, I already have the title and villain for book four. There are at least eight, maybe twelve of these for Season One. And eventually we'll get to Season Two.

So I get to tell lots of Javier stories because I can tell them faster this way.

I like that.

I do not, however, plan to turn it into any manner of love story, much to complaining chagrin of a few of you. Javier and Djamila are fire and gasoline. It's not Juliet pining over Romeo. It is two powerfully angry people trapped by circumstances and forced to do their best, systematically thinking about how to make it look like an accident.

These are all complicated people: Javier, Djamila, Zakhar, Wilhelmina. They have been thrown together by circumstance, and must deal with it. None of them can just quit and walk away. But the hatred burns deep.

And this is a dark story. Javier's usually a mouthy asshole at times, but I find his (eventual) nobility redeeming. But yeah, this one went dark.

I wanted to explore themes of identity, evil, revenge, and honor. And do so in the medium of flawed people. To think about what the real depths of space will be like in the future, when it's not a happy, clean, exciting place, but a dingy, industrial place where shit goes wrong.

The result was The Gilded Cage. I hope you will enjoy reading it as much as I did writing it.

BOOK FIVE: WILHELMINA

PART ONE

THE VOICE COMING out of the comm was such a surprise that Javier nearly set his workbench on fire with the welding laser.

"Science Officer to the bridge," Captain Sokolov growled from speakers on several walls.

Javier took the time to disarm the laser and set it down carefully. He really didn't feel the need to explain to the Chief Engineer how he managed to set off the fire suppression system.

Again.

He stood and scratched a spot on his kidneys as he stretched and weighed the urgency in the captain's voice.

The desktop was a mess. But the man had sounded a bit cross. Worse than usual, even.

Javier couldn't remember what he might have done this time to set the captain off. After all, Sykora wasn't back from her trip yet, so he really didn't have anybody to bicker with.

Too bad he couldn't figure out how to keep her gone permanently. He might even like it on this ship, regardless of his status as a highly-valued slave.

Javier considered adding a fancy sash to the basic ship uniform of slacks, undershirt, buttoned-up tunic, and occasional jacket.

They were pirates. Weren't pirates supposed to wear a fancy sash? They did in all the movies.

I wonder what uniform I could convince the crew the ancient Janissaries wore. Probably get Kianoush Buday to work up me something swanky. She'd be tickled.

Still, Sokolov hadn't asked politely. And he didn't sound like today was going to involve him using the word *please* a lot.

Javier flipped a coin in his head, studied the results, and started gathering key electronics components into his hands and sliding them into his pockets. For now, Suvi's little flitter was scattered all over the place, part of the shell here, optical sensor turret brain sitting to one side, lifter controls physically removed and sitting on a shelf.

The key components: her secondary processor, radio encryptor and transmitter, and backup memory storage, were what he wanted right now. He was in the process of upgrading the flitter's processing power, and adding more horsepower to the controller portable, so his secret AI assistant could think faster.

It was amazing what kinds of spare parts you could scavenge on a ship this size, just by paying attention.

Suvi was still a little pissed at not being a starship anymore, with all the power of a nav computer to think with and store movies and books and stuff.

But when Sokolov and his pirates had captured the two of them, Javier had just barely managed to sneak her memory and personality chip off the vessel, and then pour her into the only thing he had to hide her in, his short-range airborne autonomous remote. The one that looked like a big gray grapefruit, covered with sensors.

It wasn't his old probe-cutter, *Mielikki*, but Suvi could hide in the remote, safe from the pirates. They would have killed him if they knew about her, and turned her into a slave, too. Another slave. The flitter was as close as he could get her to starflight right now. And she had saved his ass more than once in the little flier.

"Now, Aritza," Sokolov growled from the speakers again. Apparently, he knew his Science Officer a little too well.

"Coming," Javier yelled back, stuffing things into pockets and moving to the door.

PART TWO

Zakhar Sokolov sat in his command chair and stewed.

Externally, he maintained the façade of *command*.

Aloof. Charismatic. Demanding. Durable.

The Captain.

Storm Gauntlet was on her late first shift. Normally, he would come off duty in another hour or so and go hit the tiny gym at the back of E-deck for some sweat and mobility. That wasn't going to happen today. At the same time, Javier Aritza, his Science Officer/botanist/pain in the ass slave/Centurion would have come on duty at that time.

With Djamila Sykora and Piet Alferdinck away on a mission, he was down to a very small group of centurions to stand watches, which meant he actually had to do it, instead of delegating like he normally did.

And it wasn't going to get any better.

Sokolov looked over to his administrative assistant and comm tech, Kibwe Bousaid. The man had the size and bulk to be a successful soldier or dragoon, if he had any trace of killer instinct in him. Instead, he was big, and soft, and quiet, an introvert with a passion for paperwork. And he was probably worth his weight in exotic metals as a result.

"Bousaid," he called across the bridge, waiting for the man to look up. "When the science officer and the chief engineer get here, you'll be in charge."

Bousaid nodded, powered down his station, and stood up.

Sokolov hadn't planned to interrupt what his aide was doing, but he recognized the sense of purpose the man brought to any task, so he stood as well. Bousaid would sit in the command chair, deadly serious, and be *In Command*, when he could have just kept working at his station and answered any rogue questions that came up.

Sokolov shrugged and moved to one side. They were all pirates, usually by choice, with one exception, and even Aritza had chosen to be here, when push came to shove. They all could handle their jobs with a minimum of adult supervision.

The main hatch cycled open to one side of the bridge.

Zakhar looked over and pointed at Aritza, then at his chief engineer, Andreea Dalca.

"Primary conference room," he said, moving that direction. They both stopped and turned around to head back up the hall.

JAVIER SUFFERED a moment of despair as he considered the old battered table in the conference room. The last time he had been in here for something important, he had arrived early, taken over a whole corner, and committed a petite tea ceremony while waiting for the rest of everyone to gather.

Now, it was a much smaller group, and no warning.

Javier plopped his old battered coffee mug on the tabletop and settled into a chair.

He watched Sokolov blanch slightly when he saw the other side of the mug, which, based on the amount of hot coffee inside, would currently be a beautiful young woman with green hair, and no clothing north of her belly-button.

Javier smiled.

He hadn't been the person who picked it up from the tourist shop in a brothel on *Merankorr*. He'd just found it down in the officer's wardroom about a week ago.

And kept it.

It wasn't as good as the custom team mug he had sent with Wilhelmina when she and Sykora left, but it still was very obviously his now, which kept the pixies in the wardroom and galley from stealing it when he wasn't looking.

They did that. Well, used to. Obviously the captain had worked his command magic on them at some point and made them stop. He had even said so. Not in so many words, you know. But it was all captainy magic. Bad juju.

Sokolov didn't waste any time today on polite questions or fripperies. Also, not a good sign.

"An hour ago, we received a message, transmitted from well outside the minefield, by someone who knew where the safe boundaries were located."

Inside, Javier snarled to himself, remembering all the *fun* to be had when this ship, this little private service strike corvette, *Storm Gauntlet*, had first come to *A'Nacia*, the Haunted Star, and gotten trapped in an ancient mine field like a fly in a spider's web. How much *fun* it had been figuring out how to save the ship, and her crew, when he'd really just wanted to say *I told you so*.

But in the end, they had rescued a princess from a dragon, fixed her starship, and sent her off to live happily ever after. Not bad for a bunch of pirates.

Still, there was something about the tone of the captain's voice. Something ominous and dangling, like any good bait.

Oh, what the hell.

"From whom, Captain?" Javier asked.

He wasn't going to like the answer. Might as well get it over with.

"Wilhelmina Teague."

Huh?

Apparently, Captain Sokolov had been sand-bagging, probably just to see the way Javier felt his face screwing up sideways in confusion.

Inside Javier's head, little warning buzzers and klaxons were going off as the reactor that was his brain scrambled itself and began to shut down. Or words to that effect.

Whatever.

"I'm sorry," Javier replied as he fought to keep his brain on-line. "I thought you said Ms. Teague."

"It gets better," Sokolov growled sarcastically. "She's in the smallest deep-space yacht you've ever seen. Apparently, she stole it.

"And where are Piet and Sykora?"

"They've been captured and are being held for ransom."

Well, so much for a quiet day.

PART THREE

JAVIER WATCHED his sensors and readouts like a hungry raptor. Not that there was anything he could do if something went wrong as they slowly transited the minefield back out to deep space. No, if that happened, they'd be dead so quickly they would probably never know what hit them.

He had mapped all the mines around them. Big purple triangles marked the ones that could probably gut a battleship at this range. There were a lot of those.

Out beyond that, a pretty, pink star, because that was how he thought of Wilhelmina. Not that he had really seriously considered trying his luck with the woman. His grandfather had always warned him never to chase a woman smarter than himself.

You can't catch them. And worse, what if you did?

She was one of those. Brilliant, decisive, incisive. Several different college degrees in a variety of fields. And totally freaking nuts, but at least in a good way.

She was a Shepherd of the Word. A missionary. Probably the last of them. From what he had seen, years ago, the sad, modern remainder of the order had none of the spark of the early missionaries like her.

Rip van Winkle.

At least she was nice to look at. Half a hand taller than he was. Not as tall as Sykora, but tall. Maybe a little squishier than he liked them, but five centuries in cryo-sleep would do that to you. Nothing a few months of effort couldn't fix if she wanted to.

Warm blue eyes that didn't miss anything. Cute freckles. Ready smile.

Javier smiled to himself. It would be nice to see her again.

Not that he'd been bored or lonely. He was still the new guy to many of the folks on this ship, and none of them had any misconceptions about marriage or white picket fences. But there was nobody aboard the ship that could discuss Kierkegaard or Schumpeter. And certainly not while roaring drunk.

Well, maybe Sokolov, but who wanted to get drunk with their dad?

No, it would be nice to see her again.

On the console, a single bright green light, with a helpful ping, interrupted his train of thought before it really got going.

"Aritza?" the captain asked carefully.

"You remember the range you considered safe? Sure we wouldn't trigger any mines?" Javier replied.

Sokolov nodded. "Was that it?"

"Oh, no, sir," Javier smiled innocently. "I'm eighteen percent more paranoid than you are. But we're clear."

Sokolov's glowering scowl was almost worth getting out of bed this morning, all by itself. That man was one of the few people Javier had ever met who could pull it off.

"Engines ahead three quarters," Sokolov growled. "Kibwe, keep Teague updated with our ETA."

"Aye, sir."

Javier smiled. It would be nice to see her again.

Even if she was coming with bad news.

———

THERE WERE days when Zakhar regretted not having sold Javier to an agricultural colony somewhere. Sure, they'd all be dead right now without him, but that man seemed to know exactly how to annoy people. He was like a sliver under the skin. Not painful, but something you could not ignore.

Still, today was the day to play nice. He needed the goofball even more than usual now, and was going to have to ask for the sort of favor that would forever change their relationship. Even Javier would figure that out soon enough.

After all, the man was an excellent poker player. Almost as good as his captain.

Zakhar wondered where they might have ended up if they could have been friends, instead of…whatever they were. Slavery was technically illegal on most worlds. And Javier wasn't exactly a slave. Close, but not exactly.

Technically correct was always the best kind.

Debt bondage was perfectly legal. A handful of years and Javier's debt should be paid off. If they managed to loot *A'Nacia*'s orbital graveyard properly, he might even cut that to less than one.

Zakhar considered what this would cost him personally. The two men were both Academy graduates from Bryce. Officers. Gentlemen. Anywhere else, they would be friends. Brothers in arms.

But Javier still occasionally got that look in his eyes, when he thought nobody was looking. The one that said he was visualizing most of the crew hanging from yardarms in a public square.

Perhaps not all of them. Just Zakhar and Sykora and a few others.

Today was not that day. Javier had a smile on his face, almost a goofy one. Presumably, the thought of Djamila Sykora being held prisoner and threatened with execution had cheered him up.

Zakhar sighed internally, where nobody could hear it, and considered the bait he was about to dangle in front of that man.

Even Javier would listen.

She hadn't changed.

Well, she had, but it had been to apparently spend a lot of time hitting the workout machines and doing pushups and sit-ups in the morning. Javier supposed that her time with Sykora might not have been a total waste after all. *THAT* woman was all about running for three hours in full pack before breakfast, just to wake up in the morning.

Javier was practically allergic to that level of effort. Pushing his luck was usually enough exercise. He could hit the machines and the treadmill a couple times a week and be fine.

Wilhelmina looked good. No, freaking fantastic.

This meeting could have been done on *Storm Gauntlet*. She had a conference room the right size and purpose for this sort of thing. But instead, he and Sokolov had waited for the two ships to get close enough to dock, and then crossed over to the little vessel to meet.

Just the three of them.

Normally, Javier would have been iffy about this sort of thing, but Wilhelmina had been living aboard this vessel for several days, and had a nice perfume that had worked itself into every bit of fabric visible, from the pilot's chair at one end of the room to the comfy sofa he had settled into.

Javier looked around him with a critical eye. He had lived in efficiency apartments larger than the interior of this ship. Rectangle-shaped when looking down from above, chopped at angles at belly-button level, to slope in to a roughly-pointed nose and stern, like a long, blunted diamond laying on its side. Two engine pods sticking out the back, with a jump-drive tucked between them, right behind and above the primary power unit.

Inside, a single room. Pilot station at the bow with a single chair. Sofa on one side wall, kitchenette on the other. Fold-down table and bench for eating. Storage closet on the starboard aft, head on the port aft, not far from the airlock entrance. Everything a muted seaweed green tone.

That's why it smells so nice. She sleeps on the sofa.

Javier smiled to himself, stretched out, and crossed his legs at the ankles.

Wilhelmina had greeted them both with a hug and a peck on the cheek before retreating to the pilot's chair. Sokolov ended up pulling the kitchenette bench down and perching on it rather than sitting too comfy next to Javier.

The three of them made up corners of an unhappy triangle.

"So where did she screw up?" Javier asked, to open the conversation.

He was an expert screw-up, but he also treated it professionally going in. Little miss Amazon war-babe was too spit and polish to pull off the sorts of risks he took for granted.

Wilhelmina was apparently thinking the same thoughts. She had pressed her lips together to suppress a smile.

"Perhaps a failure of paranoia," she replied.

Javier blinked. He blinked again.

Was that even possible with Sykora?

He thought about it some more. Reconsidered everything he knew about the dragoon, aware that the other two people were now staring at him.

Nope.

"Did you even make it to *Meehu*?" he asked finally.

Wilhelmina's shoulders came down. Javier only now realized how tense she had been, seated over there, when it bled out of her.

What was making her nervous? Him? Really? Weird.

"We did," she began after a brief pause, apparently to order her notes in her head. "Sykora had made some contacts with local fences to find a buyer for my old ship. The four of us: myself, Djamila, Piet, and Afia, had just finished dinner and were headed back to our hotel when we were ambushed. Djamila was stunned unconscious while the rest of us were captured."

Javier watched her stop and take a breath, eyes flickering back and forth at some bad memory.

"How did you escape?" Javier asked quietly.

"I didn't," she replied grimly. "I volunteered to deliver the ransom message to Captain Sokolov."

Javier looked around the cabin again. It smelled nice, but it wasn't the ancient explorer they had set out for *Meehu* in.

"What happened to your ship?" he asked simply.

"It's still there," she said. "We had paid for a full month docking fees, expecting to need some time to find the right buyer. But it was too slow to get here, so I hot-wired the fastest runabout I could steal and ran as fast as I could. He still thinks it will take me three or four more days to get here to contact you, so we have at least that much a head start."

"He?" the captain asked suddenly.

Sokolov had been so quiet, perched on that bench, that Javier had almost forgotten him. And he didn't look surprised. Maybe she had already told the captain part of her story, and the rest of this was for his own benefit.

"Captain Abraam Tamaz," Wilhelmina said simply.

But that look, right there, said it all.

One time, Javier had farted really loudly, the morning after an especially-bad rice-dinner-and-all-night-drinking session, and really stenched up the conference room in the middle of a centurion meeting. Sokolov got that same look on his face. Sour disgust, mixed with a dollop of angry, but holding his comments in and not venting them all over the crew.

Too busy being *The Captain*.

"You know the guy," Javier said to the captain.

It wasn't a question.

"*Storm Gauntlet*'s former Executive Officer," Sokolov replied. "A few years before your time."

"Bad feelings?"

"Tamaz wanted us to be more of a pirate operation and less of a business enterprise."

"More?"

Javier had a hard time politely wrapping his tongue around that word, considering his place in this *enterprise*.

"More," Sokolov smiled winter itself at him. "Send out a distress signal, and then massacre whoever shows up to rescue us. Raid small colonies, slaughter everyone, and steal all the hardware to sell to other colonies. *More*."

For just a moment, Javier was able to pierce the captain's veil and see the high-wire act the man had to walk every day, keeping an expensive former warship in raw materials and fresh socks, while not always having legitimate cargo to transport. The type of piracy Sokolov practiced was sometimes a lesser evil.

Javier experienced a moment of true empathy for the man. Then he carefully wrapped it up in tissue paper and put it in a box in his mind. That box he stored on a high shelf in a closet. And locked the door behind him when he left.

Sokolov and the rest of that man's crew were still all going to hang from a *Concord* Fleet yardarm one of these days. Hopefully in low gravity. Javier would see to that when he got free.

And then a little light bulb went on, just like in the cartoons.

Sykora a prisoner, being held for ransom. He and the Captain having a private conversation with Wilhelmina. *Why* the three of them were having this meeting on her vessel, instead of aboard *Storm Gauntlet*.

Witnesses. Loose tongues.

Risk.

Poker was one thing. It was a game of will and perception and luck. Javier made nice spare change off the crew playing poker, especially the engineering deck. Those people were amateurs.

Captain Sokolov was playing chess now. Probably a multi-level version Javier had seen in a bar once, with pieces representing fantasy armies on the ground, while other armies fought in the heavens and underworld. Too much like work, but some people liked it.

Everything clicked.

They wanted his help. Needed it. Absolutely relied on it to pull off whatever crazy stunt they had planned. To rescue Sykora.

Huh.

Javier actually looked both directions, like crossing the street, and then at Wilhelmina, and then Sokolov.

Time passed.

Captain had a hard look on his face. Javier imagined his own mirrored it. Wilhelmina sat perfectly still and quiet as she watched.

"I'm in," Javier said into the quiet whisper of the air systems.

Just like that.

———

ONE OF THE advantages to being The Captain, as Zakhar saw it, was generally being able to pick the field of battle. One of the disadvantages was that he occasionally forgot that behind that facile, fast-talking tongue on his Science Officer was a first-rate mind.

Something had happened to his crew when Wilhelmina Teague had first been found, trapped in cryo aboard her ancient ship inside an even-more-ancient mine field. Even before she had been rescued and defrosted.

He couldn't explain what, or why, but it had.

Sykora had become emotional and flexible about rules that used to be iron-clad. Almost human, at least for a few days. He'd never seen that in all the years he had known her, but she got over it quickly, like a bad flu.

And Javier had volunteered to walk away from enough money to possibly buy his freedom from slavery. Almost acted like a grown-up, for even longer.

The two of them had even stopped bickering long enough to make common cause.

Over Wilhelmina.

Zakhar had considered hiring Teague. It had made his ship a better place to have her around. But it had also disrupted everything in unsettling ways. He was not a man enamored of sudden, chaotic change.

He locked eyes with his Science Officer.

"I haven't asked yet," he growled.

It didn't help that the two of them tended to think along similar paths at times like this, an outcome of the years at the

Academy on Bryce, followed by active duty careers with the *Concord* Navy.

Brothers in arms.

"You will," Javier replied, now in his serious voice.

"What will I ask, Aritza?"

"We're going to go rescue Sykora. You want my help. You want me to do something nobody else on this crew can do."

"And you're in, just like that?" Zakhar asked.

"You wouldn't understand why," Javier replied coldly, as if from a great and remote mountaintop.

Zakhar agreed with that assessment.

He carefully pulled himself back from an unnecessary emotional confrontation. Aritza and Sykora had taken their hatred to a new and dangerous place because of Wilhelmina. Before that, it had almost turned into a teenage sibling rivalry. With him as the father in a sitcom.

Now they were comrades in arms themselves.

Unsettling.

"We could use words like honor, or duty," Javier continued, his tone dropping to almost a whisper. "You own my ransom, so you have both a carrot and a stick, should you choose to exercise it."

"And you'll volunteer to help rescue her, just like that, and then come back to *Storm Gauntlet* as if nothing happened? As if you weren't thinking about your own freedom and an open door? Or taking this runabout and disappearing?"

"That's right," Javier said flatly, glancing over at Wilhelmina in some random and unexplainable way.

Just what the hell had happened between Aritza and Sykora?

Zakhar had the feeling he would go to his grave with that question unanswered. Perhaps God would be willing to explain it for him, if he made it there.

Zakhar looked at the woman as well.

She was carefully not moving, as if to not disturb the emotional balance of the room. She had changed as well, but he hadn't spent that much time around her from the time she was defrosted until she had left, in order to baseline her behavior now.

Older than he had first thought. Possessed of a stillness he attributed to her being some kind of missionary, a Shepherd of the Word. Whatever that meant now, five centuries later.

Brilliant and broadly educated. Charismatic, and entertaining, and exotic all at once.

Poised.

"Wilhelmina?" Zakhar asked simply. "You're sure about this?"

She nodded once. "I am, Captain Sokolov."

"Aritza," he continued, turning now to the other thorn in his side. "Wilhelmina has asked me to send you with her back to *Meehu*, to help rescue Djamila. As you said, your return here is a matter of honor. Something between gentlemen of *Bryce*. Will you honor it?"

Javier stood up from the sofa, suddenly every inch a *Concord* officer, probably more so than he had ever been when he had worn the uniform.

"I will, captain."

Wonder of wonders.

Zakhar stood as well. Two short strides put him close to the man. He stretched out a hand.

Javier shook it.

"Good luck, Javier," Zakhar said quietly.

"Thank you, sir."

Javier considered things, smiled.

"Cavalry will be three days behind you," Zakhar said firmly. "Tamaz is not someone I would miss. Nor would the galaxy."

Zakhar turned and found Wilhelmina close.

He started to say something, but she engulfed him in a hug. Zakhar had forgotten how much taller she was until she leaned down and kissed him on the cheek.

"Thank you, Captain," she whispered in his ear.

Zakhar smiled at her and walked to the airlock door. He glanced back and watched the emotions in the room swirl.

Being a pirate was so much easier.

PART FOUR

Wilhelmina considered the scene after Captain Sokolov departed, leaving her and Javier alone.

Javier was far too nervous around her. Had been, from the first moment she could remember anything after waking up from a nap that had lasted four hundred and eighty-eight years.

She considered approaching him, initiating physical contact. She knew he found her attractive. Most men and many women did: tall, vivacious, and redheaded.

But there was an air of cold reserve around the man, like a fog, shielding him.

They locked eyes across two meters of space. Whatever it was, that remoteness, that coldness went all the way to the bottom of his soul.

In the end, she retreated, ceding him the field of battle. This was too important. The captain's chair beckoned, warm and protective. She moved next to it, but didn't sit.

Javier had taken up a spot next to the bench where Sokolov had sat by the time she had turned around.

The silence stretched, uncomfortable and taut in ways she hadn't been expecting.

Wilhelmina had spent nearly six weeks aboard *Storm Gauntlet*, recovering herself and preparing. She still felt like a butterfly emerging from a chrysalis, but the crew had treated her well, far better than she had expected, especially once she'd realized they were pirates, at least in their spare time. Six weeks had been a lot of time to recover, and to prepare.

After all, how often do you lay down to sleep, and wake up five hundred years later, hale and hearty? But the crew had accepted her, almost adopted her.

Javier had been goofy and witty, but also protective. He had seemed to like girls, but kept the space between them carefully professional, not that she hadn't considered making the effort. He was a good looking fellow, dark and well-built.

But there was a gulf now. And she hadn't said or done anything, except return.

She *had* returned without Djamila. And the wars between those two were almost legendary, to hear the crew tell it. Especially Javier's assistant, Ilan Yu.

Wilhelmina considered the emotional chasm between them.

"Did I make a mistake?" she asked finally, leaving all the linguistic options open to interpretation. He was one of the few men she had ever known who could use it as an artistic palette.

"No," Javier replied, his tone flat and hard, but not angry at her. "You did what was appropriate. What comes next will be *necessary*."

The emphasis on that last word sent a chill up her spine. This wasn't the Javier she'd known. He wore the man's shape, but there was another soul there. Something deeper, unseen. Almost malevolent.

Wilhelmina considered the fairie tales her grandmother

had told her once upon a time, in the dim recesses of history. Javier struck her as a Doppelgänger now. The shape was right, but there was a stranger sitting before her. He reminded her of no other man so much as Sokolov.

Perhaps that was what it meant to be an officer of the *Concord* Navy now. Hard men, facing a hard universe.

Had she turned Javier back into the man he used to be? Before he was happy?

"I need your help," she said finally. "Tamaz is a bad person, surrounded by bad people. I wanted to gather good men to my banner."

It almost sounded like a recruiting speech, but five months ago she had still been Shepherd of the Word, assembling good men and women in the cause of civilization. That everyone who had heard her speak that last night had been dead for hundreds of years didn't change anything. There were still monsters in the darkness, and civilization needed paladins to protect it.

Even the most unlikely of paladins.

She smiled at Javier. He had puffed up a bit, as if he could read her mind.

"The Word has been forgotten," he replied softly, almost apologetically.

"No."

She shook her head in harsh negation, eyes locked with his.

"The speakers have been forgotten, Javier," she replied, moving slowly closer to the man. "The Word will never be lost."

"Why me?"

She let go some of the tenseness in her back. They had just moved past the hard part. Javier was willing to help, to go on this quest. Wilhelmina felt like Queen Isabella, or Eleanor of Aquitaine, or Elizabeth One.

She could do this.

"Two reasons. First, Tamaz doesn't know you, and I'll be in disguise. We can get closer to him than anybody else on the crew could. Second, I wanted someone I could trust with my life."

She watched one of his eyebrows arch, rather eloquently.

"It took more than a week to get to *Meehu* in that old ship, Javier," she said. "Djamila and I had a *lot* of free time to talk. You came up a lot."

His face got even more distant and cold. He understood *what* the two women had discussed.

She sighed inside.

"I wanted to say thank you, Javier," she continued. "For letting me live. For giving me the chance to continue my mad quest. For sending me on my way with your share of the treasure, when it could have bought your freedom from *them*."

Them was obvious.

He said nothing.

Wilhelmina cursed inside, unsure how to break through, to reach him.

Moments of emptiness passed.

"Are you ready? Time is wasting, Javier," she said hopefully into the vast, emotional space.

They were close enough to dance, if he would just relax.

Some mad fire finally lit in the back of his eyes.

"If we're going to rescue Sykora, I don't even had an overnight bag, madam," he smiled up at her finally.

"I stole enough clothes for both of us, you know" she tried to leer back at him. "You won't have to slut walk home."

"That works," he said as he turned and moved away from her. "I need to grab a couple of things from the ship. Fifteen minutes and we'll be in free-flight."

It felt good to flirt with the man, even if there was some

manner of icy bulwark between them. Wilhelmina would just have to figure out how to melt it.

Djamila had never once suggested anything other than hard fire between she and Javier, and Wilhelmina knew there were no other crew members he was more than occasionally involved with. She had checked.

Could a relationship based on hatred be as fulfilling as one based on love?

Javier paused at the airlock hatch and studied her face.

He nodded to himself, turned, and disappeared through the opening.

Wilhelmina let her long legs collapse, dropping her butt into the captain's chair with an explosion of air from her lungs.

She'd had men reject her advances before, for a variety of reasons, but never once because it might get in the way of his vengeance.

She would need to work on that.

PART FIVE

IT WAS the dead of night shift.

Sleep eluded Javier. Or rather, the dreams would not let him sleep. And there was no booze aboard the little vessel that could help him relax enough to pass into darkness and stay deep.

The lights were low.

Javier didn't need to be awake. The ship was in the middle of a jump that would finally drop them at the far distant edge of the *Meehu* system, one or two jumps out from their target, but not for another three hours. If they missed the alarm clock, the ship would just sit there, waiting for someone to tell it what to do next.

It wasn't intelligent, not like Suvi, but the vessel was automated enough that someone with no experience could figure out how to make it fly. If she was as smart as Wilhelmina.

Javier sat in the pilot's seat, spun around backwards to he could rest his feet on the edge of the inflatable bed that had been hidden inside the sofa. Where he could watch Wilhelmina sleep.

Where he could brood.

With the bed inflated, there was no other room in the space, so they had ended up sharing it. It was like sleeping with your sister when you were kids. Even dead asleep, his lizard-brain kept him from rolling over and snuggling himself up against her bottom. That she slept nude didn't help. He was wearing orange sweat pants and a purple t-shirt with *Surat Thani Angels* printed on the front. Apparently, they were a professional, minor league skyball team from a far-distant sector.

Javier watched her chest rise and fall as she breathed. Even her nudity barely distracted him, which said a lot for his state of mind.

None of it good.

More than once, he considered their next hop. It would be simple enough to bypass *Meehu*, make a hard run lateral across the sector, and get back to the civilized part of the galaxy in just over a week. He wouldn't have his chickens, or his trees, but he had Suvi. They could start over, fresh.

But to do that, he would turn into the thing he despised most: a pirate.

Javier had given that man, Sokolov, his word. All Javier had now, besides Suvi, was his honor, hard-fought coin of the realm. He wasn't going to just throw that away, even in his own mind. Not for those people.

Wilhelmina had at least backed off, sensing his troubles with her feminine ways. Not that he was much more complicated than a mud puddle, according to his second ex-wife. But he wasn't himself.

They had made it through two full days of each other's company, living in each other's pockets. As honeymoons went, not bad.

Now the hard part. *Meehu Platform.*

Something woke her.

Wilhelmina rolled onto her side to look at him. The change from her normally red hair to a dark chestnut brown was jarring. It made her look like someone else, which was the goal, but it also made them strangers, sharing a bed and nothing more. That might not have been the worst choice.

"I'm sorry," she whispered.

For what was left unsaid. It could cover any multitude of sins, real or imagined. Who knew what Sykora had told her? Or rather, how much?

He nodded. It wasn't her fault he was being like this. She was just the reminder. How far they had fallen from imagined glory. What he had become. What still awaited him when he got back to *Storm Gauntlet*.

Some of the cold bled out of him. He felt his shoulders lower.

Wilhelmina patted the empty spot beside her. She stretched in distractingly-interesting ways. He noticed. She noticed.

"Come to bed," she said in a tone that left little ambiguity.

"I'm still not sure that's a good idea," he replied.

"This isn't about you, mister," she said, iron steeling her voice. "I haven't gotten laid in either six months, or five centuries, depending on how you want to count it. I have needs and you're going to help. I have no interest in anything more serious than a good roll in the hay, right now."

Javier nodded. He even smiled a little as he stood up and started to strip off his t-shirt.

This was a woman who got him.

BOOK SIX: NAVARRE

PART ONE

Abraam Tamaz smiled at the view, laid out before him like a buffet.

The room was plain. Gray walls, fluorescent lights, metal floor.

Sterile. Antiseptic.

The woman before him was not beautiful in the classical sense. She was 2.1 meters tall and built more like a man, with broad shoulders and muscles and thighs that masked the lovely, small breasts and trim waist in a cloak of false masculinity. A strong jaw and boring nose were redeemed by a spray of cute freckles. He could count nine holes in her left ear, where bangles had been removed. Her hair was the unmistakable hue of mud, clipped very short on the sides and normally standing upright in a vaguely-stylish mohawk.

Today, it was slicked back with sweat and pain.

Tamaz stepped back to get a better look at this woman, this prisoner, his prize.

She had been carefully, lovingly strapped to a modified hospital bed, her feet on his left and her head below his right hand. An intravenous drip in her left arm kept her hydrated and mildly hallucinating. Not bad, just enough to keep her tractable.

A strap was across her mouth. Not to keep her from screaming. She would never show pain. No, this was to keep her from unknowingly biting her tongue off in her agony. She might need it later.

Enough straps had been employed to keep even Djamila Sykora from moving more than two millimeters, to say nothing of getting free. He would have it no other way. Were she to escape, they would probably be forced to kill her, if for no other reason than to keep her from killing all of them.

Still, her angular, nude form was perfection itself. He paused to marvel at the taut, rippling stomach. The only men he knew with abs like that were professional models. Even the identity tattoo on the side of the ribcage closest to him was the beautiful statement of a powerful, independent woman.

She seemed to be composed of nothing but formidable muscle. Abraam Tamaz prided himself on being strong and fit, but he knew that she could out-lift him in any method, any machine he chose, as well as outrun him in full pack, and probably out-shoot him with any weapon, although that would be a matter he would have liked to test, if he could have trusted her with a loaded pistol.

Still, he lusted over this woman, all the more so because such perfection was denied to him. Oh, he could take her, but she would never know, right now. And while there were drugs he could introduce that would allow her conscious thought while he did so, she would still not give herself willingly.

At least, not yet.

Tamaz studied the wires coming from a device above her head. He traced them to little disks attached to her ears, her forehead, her neck, her nipples, her belly, her wrists, her ankles. They almost looked like tiny vines sprouting from her body. Except these were pouring electricity into her body, instead of nutrients.

Not enough to drive her mad. Oh no. Not her.

At least, not yet.

Just enough to…call it negative reinforcement. She would not come willingly. She might yet be broken to the bit, given enough time.

He was a patient man.

Tamaz nodded to the man who had been lurking nearly invisibly behind the device at Sykora's head. The man had a look of the mad scientist about him, shaved-bald head, spectacles for reading, squishy paunch, white lab coat.

In his mind, Tamaz always referred to the man as Igor, regardless of his medical degrees and schooling. After all, once you have been stripped of such honors for ethical and criminal convictions, can you really still call yourself a doctor?

Tamaz supposed that made him Dr. Frankenstein.

He always preferred Blackbeard, himself, especially once his rook-black hair began to silver in a way that seemed to make him more attractive to the fairer sex.

He looked down sourly.

Not that she would ever smile at him.

Igor turned a dial on the front of his machine. Tamaz was astounded, as always, when the nearly subconscious hum faded. The machine made him tense.

Sykora relaxed as well, but that was an end to the electricity torturing her nerve clusters. Her muscles softened from the absolute tension they had held. Even her nipples faded from their peaks.

Tamaz nodded again.

Igor opened a small vial of liquid beneath Sykora's nose. Even from here, it was foul enough to wake the dead.

Sykora stirred.

Her eyes had blinked occasionally, while under the rush of electrical pain, but that had been an autonomous function.

Now, there was cognition in there, slowly dawning.

Tamaz watched as those brilliant green eyes came to focus on the ceiling above her. After a moment, she found him standing there.

The opposite of love is not hatred. It is apathy. There is no apathy there. Now we just need to transform the passion.

Djamila Sykora came back to herself, back to him, from whatever place she retreated to in the face of his onslaught.

"It is not too late, my love," he crooned to her softly. "You have it in you to end the pain. All you must do is surrender to me."

She was not broken yet. But he knew that. The subtle way her lip and nose curled into a sneer around her gag made that evident.

But he could still try. She might yet acquiesce, before things were required to reach the ultimate stage.

Her Prince Charming, her Captain, would come soon to rescue her.

He could not bear to leave her in the hands of someone like Tamaz, where her purity might be sullied.

No, it would simply be necessary to kill Zakhar Sokolov. And to do it in front of her.

Make her watch, make her plead, make her suffer. Combined with the torture and the drugs, that should be enough to break her.

A broken Sykora would not be as good as a willing Sykora, but he could settle for half a loaf, especially one as magnificent as her.

"Sokolov is coming for you, dear Djamila," he continued, in the kind of voice you used on frightened animals.

Her eyes flared as the words penetrated her inner being.

Was that hope? Fear? Love?

Whatever it was, bringing it to the surface was just one more step on the path to breaking her, to taking her, to owning her.

Tamaz physically stopped himself from licking his lips at the thought of a pliant Sykora, offering up her core, her self, her womanness, to him.

Soon. Very soon, his vengeance would be at hand.

Tamaz nodded at Igor, silent and unobtrusive as ever. The man spun the dial back into the sixth setting.

Tamaz felt a spear of lust pass through him as her toes curled under, her back tried to arch, her nipples reached for the heavens. But never a sound passed her lips.

First I will have my revenge on Sokolov, my love. And then you.

PART TWO

Meehu Platform. An ugly, geo-synced, misshapen metal donut orbiting an otherwise-worthless planet of the same name, in an unfashionable corner of space where the *Concord* tended to bleed into vagueness and three other political entities lacked the oomph to exert their will.

Javier didn't know the place all that well, but word got around. There were always stories about a place like this.

Mostly, the tales were far more exciting and exotic than the reality would turn out to be. Pirate stations always sounded cool, but usually turned out to be rather seedy, like the bad part of a bad town where you were likely to be rolled for spare change.

The *Platform* was a few degrees better than that. Maybe. It was certainly run by a fearsome oligarchy of merchants-cum-pirate/smugglers who understood the need for a place where there were some rules, and where people could relax, without worrying about the authorities showing up. They weren't the kinds of rules you found in nicer establishments, but there were rules.

Meehu Platform's claim to fame was the level of absolute

ruthlessness behind the enforcement of the code of conduct. If you broke the rules, you paid a fine, scale dependent on your error. And you might also be banned from the station for a number of years that usually turned out to be longer than most people wanted to wait. Rarely was anyone executed. You tended to run out of paying customers if you did that.

And *Meehu Platform* was all about paying customers.

If you had a need, and the cash, almost nothing was impossible to acquire. Chickens had taken him some time, once upon a yesterday, but that was because they weren't illegal. It was simply that nobody carried them in stock.

Someone had gone off to find them and retrieve them, so they could sell them in turn to a wandering scout on a *Concord* Fleet Survey contract.

Javier smiled to himself. Everyone had assumed that he'd never been here, because they hadn't bothered to ask him.

Behind him, he could hear Wilhelmina finishing the last touches of her outfit, but he was concentrating on the station ahead of them.

I mean, how many people are crazy enough, or dumb enough to return a place like Meehu Platform *in a ship they stole from here in the first place?*

That would work to his advantage. People here were supposed to be smart. Nobody would be that dumb, so the authorities wouldn't pay that close attention if he didn't draw their attention.

Javier had spent a great deal of time, over the last few days, working on electronics. Suvi was rebuilt. Or rather, her little flitter was faster, smarter, and had enough spare storage to keep her in movies and books for about a year at the speed she usually went through stuff. A couple of centuries for him.

At the same time, Javier had exercised his paranoid demons by running through the little yacht's engines and computers. The system on the ship was stupid. He had owned smarter dogs. But he had traced every line of logic in the computer and identified all the places where a cop might look for serial numbers or other identifying marks. And a few other spots where he would have looked. And then finally he had asked Suvi to attack it from the electronic end.

All was fixed. She had even found a file that simply told a police computer where to look for a serial number that had been hand-etched with some sort of power-tool by the original owner. It didn't, anymore, after Javier had gotten into the engine well himself and flash-welded over it. Sure, a forensic specialist could probably tease the numbers and letters up, but if they were already that suspicious, he was a dead man.

"What do you think?" Wilhelmina asked invitingly.

Javier turned and looked up at her. And then remembered to pick his jaw up off the deck. Twice.

Tall. Long legs poured into pointy-toed, high-heeled boots that came up past her knees. In a color of sparkly, bright purple that was almost mesmerizing to look at. More mesmerizing than she was

Cream-colored tights that showed off the powerful thigh muscles she had obviously been working on since her long nap.

A belted tunic, dangling just past her bottom as she slowly spun in place, showing off. He would have sworn it was chamois, it had that feel. It was the color of doves in a fog.

Around her waist, a fancy sash/girdle/belt/thingee in a black so dark that is seemed to absorb light. Because he had convinced her that pirates always wore fancy sashes. Every movie agreed on that.

Glossy black leather bandoliers attached to a brass ring that rested exactly between her breasts, at the level of her nipples, and focused the eyes on the deep V of her top, straining to hold those breasts in. She had nice breasts, struggling to be free.

It took several moments to remember she had a face. A layer of makeup base had washed out all her freckles, making her seem vaguely Egyptian, an effect she heightened with the brown eye-liner and color. Blood red lips that made her look like a night creature. Mixed with the now-dark hair, she was someone else. And most men would never make it that far north, anyway, to actually see her face. He certainly didn't feel that great of a need.

"Ahem," she said, not exactly disgruntled, but obviously feeling a bit objectified as he stared at her tits.

Tough, lady. You're about to visit a station full of people who will want to kill us. Get used to being a moll.

Javier smiled. His own outfit was nowhere near as impressive. He wanted them paying attention to Wilhelmina Teague, or *Hadiiye*, as she was now going to be known.

He smiled even broader. Very few people in this sector would know enough Turkish to realize her name roughly meant *Guide*. Fitting for a one-time Shepherd of the Word.

"Very nice," he replied. "Nobody will even remember what I look like."

"He might like boys exclusively, you know," she answered tartly.

"Men are visual creatures, Hadiiye," Javier leered expansively. "Even then, he'd lust."

She blushed, even through the makeup.

Javier knew that the Shepherds took a variety of vows: poverty, obedience, chastity. That sort of thing. But she had also explained to him, lying in the darkness, covered with sweat, that those were generally more suggestions designed to keep a proper seeker on the path, rather than rules designed for monastic lifestyle. She could still enjoy a good steak, or a good tumble, but those were things for the body, not for the soul.

He disagreed wholeheartedly. They were very good for the soul.

"Stand up, you," she said finally with an impatient snap of her fingers. "I wanna see."

Javier rose.

He had refined her original vision for a blood-thirsty pirate bad-ass, but not in the direction she had intended. It was more like a troupe of Shakespeareans done in street-gang motif.

Twenty-ring lace up boots in glossy neo-leather, with curb-stomping soles and hull-metal toes. Bright red laces all the way up and double-knotted.

Knee-length britches out of dark maroon corduroy, with heavy leather combat padding along the outer edge in case someone out of a Chop-sockey movie kicked him.

Sixteen centimeter tall leather belt around his middle, with a canary-yellow sash tied around that. Much fancier than hers. Just because.

Sleeveless doublet in that same maroon corduroy, but with two rows of buttons that ran from the inside of his hips to the middle of his collar-bones. Underneath, a startlingly white long sleeve shirt.

The woman across from him had pointed out that he had the shoulders to pull a doublet off. Javier just had rarely felt the need. But this was Halloween. He could do this level of costume partying for a few days and not feel silly.

Not very silly.

Just for the hell of it, a cloth was tied around his head, with a *Neu Berne* Assault Marine logo in the middle. Sykora would appreciate that last bit. He needed a little bit of silly on his side, to balance things out before they got too dark.

A dress sword and flash pistol balanced themselves on

either side. Javier could barely use the pistol. And if it came to blades with anyone who knew what they were doing, Javier was a Christmas turkey waiting to be carved on.

Hadiiye, Wilhelmina, whistled, gesturing for him to turn in place as she had done.

"Honestly," she said with a wink as he finished. "You should consider that as a permanent look."

Javier gave her his best stink-eye scowl, but kept himself from drifting back into that *hard* place where he had been.

"It would be wasted on the rest of the crew," he said. "And you won't be around to reward me appropriately."

She blushed again. Harder this time. But didn't comment.

"So if I'm Hadiiye," she asked after a beat, "who are you?"

"I am *Navarre*," he announced with an air of dangerous menace. "The first King of Navarre, back on Earth, was an Aritza."

"I didn't know that."

"I did learn a few things in history class, lady," Javier replied.

He took a deep breath and felt the seriousness begin to take hold of him, like darkness creeping in at sunset.

"When we get there," he continued, edging ever-closer to that black place in the back of his mind. "I'm going to need you to either be dead serious bad-ass, or total bimbo, but I need you to decide right now, so I can plan accordingly. Any slip-up in front of those people gets us killed."

Javier watched her eyes and then saw her take a deep breath, almost meditatively. She rose to her full height, towering almost as far over him as Sykora did, but there were fourteen centimeter heels involved with Hadiiye. Her eyes closed for several seconds.

It was like watching ripples on a still pond as the energy

flowed outward from her belly-button to the tips of her bright red fingernails.

"I am Hadiiye," she announced in a voice that had been cast in bronze. "Killer. Assassin. Death-dealer. Commend your soul to God before you try your luck, bucko."

She had gone for bad-ass. He should have known.

Javier let a single raised eyebrow ask the next question.

"The galaxy was no safer for a single woman traveling alone five centuries ago," she purred silkily with an evil smile, just oozing *big cat predator*. "Not everyone took no for an answer. At least, not the first time."

He felt a chill in spite of himself.

PART THREE

The goons had picked them up as they entered the joint. Wilhelmina counted them.

No, damn it. Focus. Hadiiye counted them.

Five, one obviously the official bouncer, two more at the bar, and two others scattered about the room, trying to look innocent as customers.

Hadiiye did not hang on Navarre as they walked. That would have been the bimbo version of this costume.

Hadiiye was a killer. She had to act the part: blades secreted in three places, plus one on her belt; a smaller flash pistol than Navarre carried, tucked into a hidden holster, against her left kidney, where she could get at it quickly.

She was as much body-guard as gun moll here, with a dose of eye-candy designed as the second layer of distraction. Her nipples pressing against the soft cloth of her tunic certainly worked in her favor, but she honestly couldn't help herself.

This was so much fun.

Shepherds of the Word were always serious people. Constantly learning, traveling, proselytizing. They were not supposed to do things like this, dressing up in costume so they could pull off a caper on a criminal enterprise.

Hadiiye caught the appreciative looks from the five men, either staring at her chest or crotch. Navarre had been right. She would have to pay off on that bet.

But honestly, what did she know about the baser examples of men?

Well, okay, maybe that was a bit arrogant and superior, but here were several examples of exactly what the Word was intended to rectify. Hadiiye might have to kick their asses up and down the block a few times, just so Wilhelmina could preach to them, once they were properly disposed to listen to her as a person and not stare at her as a side of meat.

Wilhelmina sat quietly in one corner of her mind as Hadiiye scowled at the men. They were seeing her undressed and probably bent over one of the tables in this restaurant, with them taking turns.

She envisioned them hanging from hooks in an abattoir.

Apparently, they picked that attitude up as she moved.

Javier walked up to the bar and leaned against it.

No, damn it. Navarre.

A flunky appeared from a door behind the bar, cold and arrogant as he considered these *tourists* who had obviously wandered into the wrong joint.

Navarre could handle him. Hadiiye turned to study the rest of the space. And the men subtly adjusting themselves as if violence was imminent.

Because seriously, if you needed five to take on the two of us, your boss needs to hire better goons.

And that was what they were. Goons. Second-rate, muscled thugs guarding a restaurant that specialized in French cuisine. On a station dedicated to being a criminal marketplace. In the middle of nowhere.

Hadiiye smiled to herself, then let it encompass the men

around her. Once upon a time, a young Shepherd named Wilhelmina had taught close combat techniques to younger students, mostly girls, preparing them to go out into the oh-so-dangerous galaxy and preach the Word. She had the reach for it, too, with legs longer than some people.

Behind her, the bartender grunted something rude.

Navarre responded in French, which apparently surprised the bartender almost as much as it did Hadiiye.

"I don't care what you think, peasant-boy," Navarre growled softly. "Your job is to send a message to Captain Tamaz. If you can't handle that, I'll have one of these puppies here do it, instead."

Around them, the punks tensed, but that was the way hackles came up at being insulted, rather than about to attack. Indignant shock.

"What message?" the bartender asked with an accent better suited to one of the harsher slums of Paris. How had he gotten out here, so far from Earth?

But then, how had Hadiiye? They were all far gone from home.

The assassin fixed her steely eye on each of the men in turn. It wasn't exactly a dare. It was worse. It was a woman simply laughing at them as the junior varsity.

"My name is Navarre," the once-and-future Science Officer said condescendingly. "I want to talk about the woman from Neu Berne. He'll understand. Right now, we are going to have dinner at Galileo's. Good day."

Navarre appeared in the corner of her eye, already moving towards the door at a sharp clip. Hadiiye smiled once more at her prey and followed the man out the door.

"How DID you know where to go to find him?" Wilhelmina asked. She was still Hadiiye, but they were in a lovely bistro specializing in traditional Italian peasant food. There was enough music and chatter to keep their conversation private as long as they were careful.

The food was excellent.

"While we were inbound, I made a few calls. You were in the shower," Javier replied.

Except it wasn't Javier. It was still *Navarre*, a hard, cold, pirate son-of-a-bitch that looked more like the man who had stood on her deck with Captain Sokolov than the goofball who had awakened her from a magical sleep.

At least she had finally gotten her kiss.

"You know people at *Meehu*?" Wilhelmina was shocked.

He hadn't mentioned anything. She had been prepared to wing it, knowing they had a few days to scout before Sokolov would arrive.

This creature named Navarre wasn't waiting.

"I've been through here before," he replied, in a tone that didn't suggest further questions on the topic.

"So what's your plan, Navarre?"

She was still a little lost in this century. Certainly, humanity hadn't changed much. But she'd never been a criminal element before. Fun, but a bit unnerving. Navarre was an interesting, if unsettling companion.

"We have a two or three day head start," the hard man across from her replied. "He won't start getting prepared for Sokolov just yet, probably figuring that the captain couldn't react so quickly. We're going to get close to him first, find his weaknesses, and exploit them."

Navarre leaned forward and put both elbows on the table, resting his chin on crossed fists. His eyes grew even harder.

"It will probably be necessary to kill people before we leave this station, Hadiiye. Are you at peace with that?"

"I think so."

"No," he replied flatly.

It was the tone that chilled her. Up until now, this had been a game of dress up, for a party. She sensed a line suddenly drawn in the sand at her feet.

"*No?*"

"You will either say *yes*, or you will stay on the ship while I handle this. I have to trust you completely, unquestioningly. Pick. Right now."

The last several days were gone, just like that. The last six weeks. The friendship. The comradery. Staying up late and fooling around. Everything.

Gone.

Doppelgänger.

There was no Javier. Only Navarre. Where had he come from? Would she ever see Javier again?

Already, she missed him.

"I trusted you with my life," she said quietly. "My soul."

"No. Sykora did that. You were just the result."

Huh?

Wilhelmina thought back to the long conversations with Djamila, over tea, listening to the ancient ship chug through the darkness while Piet and Afia slept. She had missed something. Something critical between those two, Javier and Djamila.

Lovers in hatred.

Wilhelmina considered her options.

The Word conveyed the value of all lives. At its very bottom, the cornerstone of Rama Treadwell's teachings was the very egalitarian nature of happiness. All beings deserved the freedom to define and obtain happiness on their own terms, in their own way, free from censure.

Thus had she been taught. Thus had she taught.

And yet…

Sophisticates frequently fell into their own logical trap: the *Fallacy of Pacifism.* They forgot that the Vow of Peace contained within it the promise of violence in defense of others.

Shepherds of the Word were expected to engage with their words, but they were also equipped to use their hands, if all else failed.

Wilhelmina looked around the room once, aware that Javier was waiting for an answer. To an outsider, it would look like Hadiiye actively looking for threats to her being. But this was much deeper.

There were no tourists here. Not in the sense of fat, happy, middle-class travelers on an adventure. That kind did not come to *Meehu.* Even accidentally.

Instead, there were kids, folks barely past their teens, who had either run away, or been chased out. There were middle-aged people who had lost it all and had to start over. There were older people trying to hang on to something, facing only a cold and lonely death ahead.

Very few of the people she could see here probably intended this as their destination, their lot.

But then, who did?

Wilhelmina framed the words, passed down from Rama Treadwell and his intellectual descendants a very long time ago, but Hadiiye spoke them aloud.

"Paladins are men and women of the *Sword*, Navarre."

There. Commitment.

I will kill people for you, for Djamila, for Sokolov. I will use violence to try to make the galaxy a better place, not by imposing my order upon it, but by using my will to thwart would-be conquerors, bad men, villains.

Navarre studied her for several moments silently before he drew a breath and nodded.

For a moment, she saw a depth of pain in Javier's eyes she had never imagined existed. Something terrible and bitter. Obviously, he was good at hiding things from people.

Would it better to let it lie, or help him heal? Would he welcome the suggestion?

A change came over Navarre as he glanced to his right over her shoulder. Subtle, but critical.

Hadiiye shifted her weight invisibly and let one hand fall off the table to rest close to a blade balanced for throwing, hidden in her right boot top. Something prickled in the air, like the smell of ozone.

"Captain Navarre?" a man asked carefully.

Hadiiye looked about, but nobody else was paying attention. She glanced back at the figure.

Oily, in a slippery way. Well-dressed man in dark pants and matching jacket. Businessman who knew how to wear the suit, instead of the goons at the other restaurant who let the suits wear them. Hair cut short, brown on top and graying on the edges. Conservative and quiet.

Hard, but in a deadly, accountant kind of way, rather than being a killer.

Not like her.

Across the table, Navarre relaxed a touch, perhaps from absolute zero to merely liquid nitrogen.

"Indeed," Navarre said, gesturing to the table. "Please, join us. Have some wine. Let us talk like civilized beings who find themselves at an uncivilized crossroads."

There was the Javier she remembered. Smooth, charming, eloquent. Even hiding behind that hard face.

These bastards had no clue what they were up against.

The man nodded appreciably and pulled a chair out with one hand, all manners in a place that could barely spell the word, let alone practice it.

Hadiiye felt his eyes pass over her once. Wilhelmina would have smiled. Hadiiye scowled instead, intent on her role as a moll, a sidekick.

A killer.

She felt him dismiss her, barely lingering on her cleavage, before he turned his attention fully on Navarre.

"I do not believe we have met before, Captain Navarre," the stranger said carefully. "My name is Marcas Almássy. I work as an agent for Captain Tamaz. I understand you wish to speak with him."

Navarre had lowered his hands and leaned back from resting his chin on his knuckles. He reached out now and took hold of a half-filled wine glass as a waiter materialized with a second glass and a new bottle.

Moments of silence passed as the waiter expertly cracked the new bottle, poured, and disappeared, without a word spoken. Obviously, this wasn't the man's first visit. Good to know.

"I understand," Navarre finally said, slowly, carefully. "That Captain Tamaz has recently come into possession of a person. A woman, exceptionally tall, formerly of *Neu Berne*, now a freebooter."

Almássy paused, sipped his wine appreciably, and considered the tableaux.

"And where might you have heard something like that, Captain Navarre?"

She watched Javier, *Navarre*, lean closer, conspiratorially.

"Someone talked," he almost whispered with a chilly smile. "Someone always talks."

Hadiiye held her breath as the energy rippled between the two men. She remained aware of every patron and every wine glass in view, confident that the two men with her would cover her blind flanks if something happened. Both were professionals.

The room remained amateur.

"And your interest in the woman?" Almássy inquired with a smile.

Crocodiles might learn something from this man.

"Entirely personal," Navarre replied succinctly. "Old business. Unfinished."

For a moment, she watched all of Javier's hatred bubble to the surface. There were actors who could probably fake that sort of thing, but they were few and far between. And they would be hard-pressed to match something like this. Perhaps only a master Shakespearean could manage.

"And were you interested in negotiating a bounty for her?"

Hadiiye nearly choked at the price the man quoted. It was a significant proportion of the extravagant fortune Sykora had thought she might get for the ancient freighter with the amazing history.

Almássy and Navarre leaned close, two old merchants at the bazaar, getting down to brass tacks. She wondered if the man owned one of those old-fashioned accountant hats, all bill and no lid.

He had that feel to him.

"Oh, no," Navarre smiled, catlike. "I was much more interested in obtaining front row seats when you executed her. That would satisfy me. And my backers."

"Backers?"

Hadiiye saw the man's concentration crack for a second of utter confusion as the implications of the word settled on him like a winter mantle.

Navarre wasn't a lone wolf who wouldn't be missed if something happened to him. Others might inquire. Unknown others. Potentially dangerous others.

She considered it a masterful job of misdirection, until she saw the light in Navarre's eyes. If a supernova was white hot summer heat, this was the exact equivalent in winter.

The accountant saw it as well. He retreated, emotionally as well as physically, leaning back as far as his chair would comfortably allow.

Moments passed.

Navarre considered the man as bobcat might consider a field mouse.

"I think," Almássy responded finally, "that you would be better served to discuss such a matter with Captain Tamaz directly, Captain Navarre."

"I suspected as much."

"Perhaps you will be able to come to the club, Sevenoaks, this evening? Captain Tamaz will be handling some business there in about six hours. I am certain he will be quite interested in making your acquaintance."

Navarre rose slowly from his chair, his hand extended. Almássy did the same.

"I look forward to it, Mr. Almássy," Navarre said. "Until then."

And then the man was gone.

The emotional power of the room dropped precipitously, even as the space seemed to grow warmer.

They were alone again.

Hadiiye smiled tightly at her partner.

"Navarre, that was a most amazing bluff."

He fixed her with a cold stare.

"Bluff?"

PART FIVE

THE LITTLE, unnamed, stolen ship was a useful base while they stayed at *Meehu Platform*. For the time they would be here.

Javier scanned the single room once, taking note of several little things he had left, precisely located, that would have been moved by someone rifling the place for clues to his identity. It was second nature when he had to deal with people. Any people. Even ones he liked. In addition, he had left Suvi's sensors on, so she would have flashed a red light at him if anyone had come in.

The space was still secure. He entered, the hard woman one step behind him.

Javier took off Navarre like an old, comfortable cloak and hung him by the airlock hatch, along with the belt holding the sword and pistol. The ship felt warm, almost enough to leech the cold from his bones and soul.

He turned to find her standing in the middle of the room as the hatch closed.

They studied each other, across a gulf far greater than it had been when they left.

"It's safe to be you," he said.

It wasn't an apology, but it was headed in that direction.

"Are you you?" she replied.

Javier considered any number of responses, some of them tart, some angry, a few goofy.

It was a fair question. It deserved a fair answer.

"Close enough. For now," he replied.

These two women had taken him to his dark places. It wasn't her fault. Sykora had started him down that road when they met almost a year ago. Wilhelmina when she first came into his life, and then again when she came back.

"So what do we do now?" she asked, looking unsure for the first time since they had left *Storm Gauntlet*, days ago.

"Now we sleep," he replied, popping buttons and taking off the doublet. "It will be a long night, with a bunch of punks who like to think they're tougher than everyone else by staying up all night drinking shots of engine coolant."

"Really?"

"Really," he said, starting to unlace the boots. "After a nap, more food to absorb the booze."

"What about Djamila?" she asked evasively.

"We don't know where they're keeping her," he replied. "Or how to get her out."

He paused, looked up, fixed her with a hard gaze.

"Yet. We do know she's still alive."

"You're sure?"

"Yes," Javier replied. "He would have offered to sell me footage if they had killed her already."

She took a step sideways and sort of collapsed into the captain's seat.

"So we'll waltz in there?" she asked. "Just like that?"

"Unless you know a way to hack into their security systems and steal all the information we need," he replied, tugging a boot off.

"And Tamaz will fall for it?"

Javier smiled at her. It was a brutal smile. His mind was in a brutal place.

"If he doesn't," he said, "then we're dead."

"And you plan to sleep at a time like this?"

His smile became more rueful.

"I'm surprised you aren't better accustomed to sleeping whenever you got the chance, as slow as that old barge of yours was."

"That was different," she replied, pulling off her own boots and making fists with her toes. "That was boredom. I was never risking my life."

"Wilhelmina," he said sharply. "You were risking your life every time you jumped into hyperspace. Every time you got out of bed. Maybe you should consider how risky this universe is and start paying attention."

"I am paying attention," she shot back, edges of panic creeping into her voice. "But three months ago I was a missionary. Now I'm an assassin. And I have nobody but you to get our mission done. I'm scared."

Javier considered the woman sitting there.

For the last several hours, she had been merely a piece of furniture to maneuver around. An art object that happened to move. He had gotten so lost in himself again that he forgot people around him.

They had feelings. Wishes. Dreams. Fears.

That many years in deep space, alone but for a clutch of chickens, had helped smooth over some of the rough spots, but there were still holes. Landmines he occasionally stepped on. Less so now, but still there.

Fighting a war with Sykora had both sharpened those issues, and made them recede a bit. He had stopped being introspective when he had a foe worth the name.

Now he had Wilhelmina, who might be a…what? A friend? A comrade? A lover?

All of those. None of them. Something. Nothing.

He stood up and held out a hand. She rose as well and took it mutely.

Javier considered his options.

"You trusted me with your life," he said, feeling the warmth of her skin. "Even when you didn't know it."

He was close enough to her to smell the underlying flowers of her perfume that suffused the room.

She looked down at him, confused, and nodded.

"I'm going to do the same," he said. "There is a secret that is worth my life, if Sykora and Captain Sokolov ever find out."

He watched her eyes grow a little bigger, but she remained silent.

Javier smiled. It was warm this time. Maybe for the first time in weeks. Months. Years. Lifetimes.

"Before I was a slave," he said. "I was an explorer, doing survey work for the *Concord* Navy on the far fringes of civilized and terraformed space."

He studied her face. She had withdrawn some, not so much distant as closed. She nodded again, as a placeholder while he spoke.

"I had a lovely, little probe-cutter for a ship," he continued. "It had been retired out of *Concord* service, demobilized, and was destined for the breaker yard. I got it cheap, fixed it up, and reprogrammed the AI aboard to be much more human and interesting than she had been when she was in the fleet."

Javier felt a pang of anguish and rage stab him in the guts as he thought of his lost starship, of *Mielikki*. Of how much he owed Zakhar Sokolov and Djamila Sykora. He did not, could not, let the emotion show.

"When I was taken by Sokolov's crew," he continued. "I told them I had destroyed all the personality and programming circuits. I lied."

She blinked in surprise. Obviously she had heard part of that story at some point. Probably from Sykora.

Vast oceans of emotions and questions played across her face as she stayed perfectly silent.

"Instead," Javier said, "I smuggled her out in a bucket of chicken feed, and then poured her into the only thing I had that was remotely like her old home."

"Her?"

He pointed at the autonomous sensor remote, resting on a shelf where he had placed it when he finished all the upgrades he could manage without building her a bigger body.

"Wilhelmina Teague, I would like to introduce you to my former first mate, my comrade in surveying, my friend. Suvi, please say hello to Wilhelmina."

On the shelf, lights clicked on and the sixteen centimeter, gray, grapefruit-looking globe rose into the air with the faintest of hums.

Because he was holding her hand, Javier felt the sudden surge of adrenaline as Wilhelmina's muscles clenched.

Her era held nothing like the AIs of the present day. There had been smart systems, extremely autonomous and capable, but they did not compose music. Or write poetry.

They did not dream.

"Doctor Teague," Suvi said warmly. "It is my pleasure to finally get to meet you. I have been looking forward to this for so very long."

PART SIX

She was back to being Hadiiye.

Javier had explained how to wear the identity like a costume, intricate and realistic, but never once exposing your inner self while playing the role.

She wondered if she had ever seen Javier not playing some role. She considered asking Suvi sometime, when he wasn't around.

Sevenoaks turned out to be a noisy nightclub, located well away from the other two establishments she had visited with Navarre. It wasn't a pretty place, filled with well-dressed folks showing off in a complicated mating ritual.

No, it was much rougher, filled with crew off of various ships docked at the station, perhaps at a two or three to one ratio, male to female, plus a variety of what were obviously locals and professional entertainers, here eight or ten to one female.

The first person to grope her bottom in this place was going to end up eating teeth.

Just for good measure, Hadiiye pasted a hostile snarl on her face and followed Navarre as he slowly made his way through the press. It was not a full rugby scrum, but there was unavoidable-but-polite jostling. Her height and obvious attitude problem helped clear her path.

Away from the dance floor, the crowd thinned out. Sevenoaks wasn't particularly cavernous, but it made good use of space, with a bar along each side wall, and a series of four rising levels, like steps for giants, climbing towards the back of the club.

She could see booths up there, filled with older patrons, while the kids were down here. Apparently, there was a kitchen around here as well. She saw several people eating dinner, or at least snacks more complicated than instant bar food.

Not that she could hold another bite at this point. But she was good for drinking, especially with men who had never gotten drunk with a missionary before. In some places, there was nothing to do but drink with the locals. You got to be good at holding it.

Almássy, the accountant, rose from a booth above them and back a few tiers as they approached the rear of the club. There wasn't a toll gate here, but several bouncer-looking goons in black muscle shirts made it obvious where the invite-only section began.

Seeing dancers and patrons move against that was like watching waves lap at the beach, with clean, dry sand beyond them.

Navarre walked right up to the bouncers. She stayed a step and a half back and a half step to his left, where she could see over his shoulder, prepared for trouble.

The music wasn't that loud, but she watched Navarre gesture silently to one of the bouncers as Almássy approached, instead of speaking. The man got a nod from the accountant, nodded back, and they were on dry land.

It was quieter here, as well. Wilhelmina would have

appreciated the architectural design that went into the ceiling and load-bearing pillars to shelter them from most of the noise. Hadiiye concentrated on people, mostly seated, mostly ignoring her.

The crowd here was different, as she had thought, but not really older. More mature. Perhaps more professional. Much more dangerous. These were captains, and senior officers from various ships, mingling with bankers and fences, if the suits were any clue. Hard men and women, doing deals.

There were no working girls back here.

Almássy shook hands with Navarre and ignored her for the most part. She followed the two men up a set of shallow stairs to the top-most tier, against the back wall of the club.

From the elevation, she guessed there was an entire set of suites or conference rooms below them, but she didn't know this place well enough to guess if they were cribs for a brothel or conference rooms for more complicated, private deals.

Hadiiye didn't care nearly as much as Wilhelmina might have.

They were led to a horseshoe-shaped booth on the fourth tier with the best view. She recognized Captain Tamaz from her previous *encounters*, as well as Adam Erckens, the man's first mate.

Wilhelmina hadn't really had a chance to study Captain Tamaz before, and certainly hadn't paid attention to the sorts of detail Hadiiye required now.

He was tall, even sitting down. She would have guessed he had a centimeter on her if they were both in stocking feet. His black hair was long and tied back in a tail. It had streaks of silver that would have made him distinguished, but for the cruel mouth and harsh eyes.

Captain Tamaz was clean-shaven, but she could already see a shadow on his jaw. This was a man who might need to shave twice daily.

Hairy men didn't do it for either her or Wilhelmina.

Erckens sat next to his captain in the black leather booth. If Tamaz captained a rugby team, and he had that look, Erckens was the muscle in the middle of the scrum. There was nothing soft about the man, from the auburn flattop to the scarred hands resting on the tabletop.

He had the build of a man who spent a lot of time and energy on the right nutrition, the right drugs, and the requisite number of hours at the gym daily.

Fanatic, in all the wrong ways.

Hadiiye's tits sheltered her. None of the three men at the table appeared to even notice she had a face as she approached. The one woman sitting with them looked closer, but said nothing.

She was a stranger, dressed like a banker but still in good shape, if thickening with age. Hadiiye would have guessed her to be in her well-preserved fifties. She could see the older woman's beauty slowly aging, like the best wines, even as she wore little makeup and kept her hair buzzed to perhaps three or four millimeters long.

Her eyes, though. They had the intelligence of an alpha predator, but the warmth of a human, something missing from the three men here. Four, with Navarre.

Tamaz nodded, mostly at Navarre.

"Captain Navarre," he said carefully with a semi-formal nod. He did not rise, but the body language suggested it diplomatically as he gestured for them to join his party.

Dominance games. Two springboks about to joust for supremacy. Local boys unsure of the stranger and willing to play nice for now. At least until he showed weakness. Sharks waiting patiently.

Wilhelmina was aghast, deep inside, as Hadiiye used her well-honed perceptive skills so ruthlessly.

Tough.

"Captain Tamaz," Navarre replied, equally politely.

Bodies shifted around, making a space for Navarre to sit next to Almássy, with Erckens between him and Tamaz.

The woman chose to slide out of the booth and stand.

"Tamaz," the banker said. "I will check my inventory and get back to you in a day or so. I'm sure we can deal."

She looked up and eyed Hadiiye from close up, almost a head and a half shorter but massing a similar amount.

She nodded with the ghost of a smile, and departed without another word.

Hadiiye could have slid in, but chose to remain standing.

Bodyguards, professional ones, didn't limit their movement like these men did. She could probably successfully assassinate Tamaz, if she was suicidal. There were enough guns around her that she'd never make it out alive.

That wasn't necessary. Yet.

For all the noise on the dance floor, it was quiet enough to talk here. Hadiiye suspected a sound-dampening field, but didn't bother looking for it. It would be concealed, along with pop-up stunner turrets a bar like this would certainly invest in.

"I do not believe we have met," Tamaz said, dangling his tone like bait.

Useful, if you wanted to catch a megalodon.

"I rarely work this sector, Captain Tamaz," Navarre replied. Not evasive, but not particularly descriptive. "This was a special trip."

His smile could have sliced bread.

"And your interest in the woman?"

Navarre's smile turned winter.

"I owe that woman more pain than you can possibly imagine," Navarre purred.

"Professional," Tamaz asked, "or personal?"

"Or?"

"I see," Tamaz said succinctly. "Almássy tells me you inquired about a front-row seat for her execution."

"She's cost me too much money," Navarre said. "I can't afford to buy her from you outright."

"Oh ho, so it is professional."

"No," Navarre replied. "With Sokolov, it's professional. With her, it's very much personal."

A single raised eyebrow asked the obvious question. Navarre nodded, warming slightly to the man.

Hadiiye tensed, wondering if this was the point where things would get out of hand, or whether Javier was about to change sides.

Did he have a side?

"They cost me a very expensive, very custom ship."

"I don't remember you, Captain Navarre," Tamaz said sternly. "And I would."

It was Navarre's turn to raise an eyebrow.

"You served with Sokolov? With Sykora?"

She watched Tamaz lean back and smile, almost preening.

"I was *Storm Gauntlet's* Executive Officer," the man announced. "Before I decided to go make my own fortune five years ago. They dreamed too small for me."

"Five years?" Navarre asked. "Then my backers would have no beef with you. Only them. Him, mostly."

"So you aren't really that interested in the woman?"

Hadiiye saw something in the man's eyes. She wasn't entirely sure what it was. Wilhelmina might have discounted it. Another man would have missed it entirely.

Hadiiye was a woman. A hard, brutal, lethal woman. Keyed up for violence and studying all the men about her as victims in waiting. But still a woman.

There was something oddly possessive about the way the

man spoke, the way he smiled. Something at odds with the situation. Both Javier and Navarre would miss it.

Hadiiye decided to gamble.

"You could always let me have her," she said with a slow drawl, just loud enough to be heard, just cold enough to convey a very painful point.

Every head turned her direction. Eyes met hers and stayed, for the first time, instead of wandering down her front.

She had just become a person instead of an object.

The tension shifted, bled sideways. Navarre scowled, blinked, processed, grinned. *Good.*

Tamaz studied her closely. His eyes took her in entirely, from the high-heeled fighting boots to the bronze-ringed gap that showed the shadows of her breasts as she breathed, to the long, long arms ending in blood red nails.

She smiled, catlike at him, watched him lick his lips unconsciously. *Better.*

"Interesting," Tamaz said.

Either he was a better poker player than Javier, or he had just bought the identity of Hadiiye.

She wondered if either Javier or Navarre realized how much Tamaz was in love with Djamila Sykora.

"After dealing with Sykora," Navarre said into the silence. "I went and got my own version."

"Is she as good?" Erckens suddenly spoke up, having been silent until now. He had a tenor voice. It might have been pleasant, if it wasn't dripping with frat-boy innuendo and lust.

"Maybe," Navarre said. "She's killed everyone I've wanted her to, so far."

Maybe, Navarre? You don't think Hadiiye could take Sykora?

Wilhelmina spoke up from her quiet corner, offered a memory of Djamila working out. The muscles rippling as she lifted huge weights, did hand-stand pushups against a bulkhead, punished the sparring dummy Wilhelmina held for her.

No, probably not. You three, however, would be meat.

Hadiiye settled for a predator's smile. Big cat.

She *had* killed everyone Navarre had asked her to. That turned out to be nobody as yet, but perhaps he would demand Tamaz and the other two be first. That would please her, after experiences with these men that she would never tell Javier or Djamila.

"Killing Sykora isn't really necessary," Tamaz purred.

Again, that soft undertone. Wilhelmina, the Shepherd of the Word, spoke up, offered all the experience of a doctorate in human psychology. Helpfully pointed out the set of the eyes, the posture, the way the lips held that smile.

He wasn't going to kill her, but he was never letting her go. He was going to break Sykora. Shatter her. Make it impossible for her to say no to him.

That would be enough. Tamaz was a glass-half-full man with Sykora. Not just simple conquest, but also willful acceptance. Something Djamila would never give him willingly.

There was no more dangerous creature in the world that a thwarted lover plotting his revenge.

Wilhelmina wondered about Javier's posture. It was different, but not different enough. The opposite of love is apathy, not hatred. Javier was not apathetic here.

Navarre watched Tamaz and the others for a second. He nodded, mostly to himself.

"In that case, gentlemen," Navarre said. "We probably can't do a deal. My apologies for interrupting your evening."

He began to slide out of the booth, but Tamaz stopped him.

"Actually, Captain Navarre," he began, much more politely. "We might be able to. Sokolov ought to be here in another few days. We can certainly find a happy common cause around his death."

He dangled the bait skillfully.

Hadiiye watched the play of emotions across Navarre's face. She knew Javier well enough from across a poker table to see how much of it was false detail. Hatred. Hope. Vengeance.

Navarre cocked his head.

"Sokolov's coming for her?" he asked, voice dripping with anticipation. His smile gained several degrees of warmth.

"I sent a messenger to draw him in," Tamaz replied. "She had a slow ship, so we have a bit of time to prepare."

"She?"

"One of Sykora's crew. She'll scamper home and undoubtedly bring the cavalry, like it was some boring melodrama. They will expect a trap. I will serve them up one they can escape. They will rescue Sykora. I'll use her to kill them all."

Tamaz was preening again. Butter would not melt in his mouth right now.

Navarre reached out a hand and grabbed the glass of wine that had been in front of the woman banker. He made a production of toasting Captain Tamaz with it.

"To vengeance," Navarre said seriously.

The others scrambled to grab their glasses and rattle them together awkwardly. "To vengeance."

Hadiiye scanned Tamaz and his crew expectantly. They might have Sykora, but they were toasting retribution with Javier Aritza, even if he was portraying the role of Captain Navarre.

Who was doomed here?

BOOK SEVEN: DJAMILA

PART ONE

It wasn't *Mielikki*, but it was still an improvement over that short-range airborne autonomous remote Javier had hidden her in when the pirates first captured them. A girl could stretch her legs out in here.

Suvi completed an inventory of her upgraded suite of toys. The new remote was eighty-three percent faster to process and had nearly forty-three times as much non-volatile memory. Javier had even added a whole library of new movies and musicals for her to watch when she had time.

The shell had been reinforced, as well. After she had cracked her egg killing the bad man, the remote's frame had never been the same. She could compensate, but having to was a pain. The new shell was much tougher, with a layer of charcoal gray painted hull metal padded underneath with nearly a centimeter of good sprayed-foam material, double wrapped in cloth. She was hurricane-proof now, too, instead of just rain-proof. Bigger batteries, more lift potential, refined sensors.

It almost made it worth it.

Still, she missed being a starship. She'd have to convince

Javier to buy or steal her a ship one of these days, upgrade the hardware, and pour her soul into it. Oh, to feel the solar wind on her face again.

At least she'd finally met Dr. Teague. Finding out Javier had given that woman all of their reward money from the mine field treasure above *A'Nacia*, that he'd added years to their sentence of servitude, that had hurt. She had been all set to hate the woman, especially after finding out that now she wanted their help to rescue the big, mean dragoon, Sykora.

I mean, really, the nerve of some people.

But Wilhelmina had turned out to be good people. Really nice. Probably good for Javier in ways Suvi couldn't manage, unless they built her an android body with big boobs.

Pygmalion be damned. A girl could dream.

Dinner and talk and stories and plans, plus a lot of food. Javier obviously trusted Wilhelmina with his life, with both their lives, so she must be good people. Really nice, too.

And now, a costume party. Well, for the organics. Actually, no, her too. Nobody would realize that the little remote had a person inside.

And other surprises.

Suvi cycled her attention back down to the new entries in her encyclopaedia entitled *Q-section*. Javier had added some new capabilities when he updated the hull of the new remote. It wasn't her old dorsal twin pulsar turret on *Mielikki*, but she could still take down a moose with the little pop-up pulse turret she had now.

Were there any moose in space?

Suvi made a note to update her xeno-biology and seeding histories to look for programs to introduce large ungulates on terraformed planets. Or, alternatively, to locate bioequivalent creatures on non-seeded worlds. You never knew when you'd need that kind of information handy.

Q-ship. A very boring-looking freighter in a war zone, sailing happily along as bait for an enemy raider. Armed and armoured, but hidden. Prepared to absorb lots of damage. All set to sink the poor bastard who thought he was all that and a bag of chips.

Suvi envisioned dancing a happy jig before she climbed down into the flight seat of her little flitter, at least in her mind, and started the power-up sequence to bring her little assault fighter on line.

Scanners: active. Currently tracking one target: Javier, currently costumed as Captain Navarre, with a little ping transmitter in his belt-buckle that apparently even Wilhelmina/Hadiiye didn't know about.

Flight systems: warming up. I can outrun a cheetah. And out-marathon a saluki. And out-climb a Stellar's Sea Eagle.

Fear me, I am awesomeness itself.

Batteries: ninety-nine point three percent. No solar power around here to recharge, so I'll have to rely on standard indoor fluorescent lights. Estimate nineteen days to critical discharge, two if I use the guns on anything. Assume trouble.

She made another note to have Javier relocate the standard plug-jack closer to her waldo claw, so she could find a power socket and get to one hundred percent without relying on him.

Cavalry needs to be able to cavalry, damn it.

PING!!!

Suvi nearly dropped her iced tea. Well, she envisioned one in her hand so she could almost drop it. Then she added a cup-holder on her console, to hold her new glass, and finished her power-on sequence. Javier would only push that button when he was ready for her to follow them to the bad guy's lair. And since Wilhelmina/Hadiiye didn't know about it, that meant Suvi needed to come running.

She popped up off the bench, oriented herself with one last hard ping of the little runabout's interior, and flew her nose carefully into the airlock control button.

She needed a bugle. Well, an external sound system so she could play the bugle.

Cavalry needed to cavalry.

She added it to the list.

He's gonna owe me big after this, anyway.

HADIIYE WAS astounded at the amount of alcohol the three man had put away while she and the accountant had watched. It was staggering. Seven empty bottles of the hard stuff were lined up carefully along the edge of the table. Dead soldiers awaiting proper interment.

About midway through that performance, someone had decided to send a goon over to protect Captain Tamaz while he got really, really drunk with his new friend, Navarre. Hadiiye kept one eye on the newcomer, just as he watched her.

Insurance policy, really.

The new guy, the body guard/bouncer, was one of the biggest humans Wilhelmina had ever laid eyes on. Dark brown hair, nut brown skin, nearly black eyes. He would have been half a head taller than Sykora, were she here, and massed her by at least four stone, maybe five. Wilhelmina was even more amazed when the man moved.

It was obvious that the man had studied ballet at some point. He was too big to be any good, but she couldn't think of a single martial art she had studied, on any of the worlds she had ever visited, that would teach you how to keep yourself so perfectly poised and centered as you moved. Plus, she recognized the way his hands and feet moved.

Those skills had been pounded into an eight-year-old version of her, once upon centuries ago.

So, trained as a dancer, moves like a jaguar. Callouses on his hands from striking things repeatedly. Close in, he would be murder. Stay far away and shoot at him instead.

He looked like a breaking-boards-and-heads kind of guy.

Hadiiye wondered if he had ever studied one of the descendants of Aikido or Judo. She smiled to herself.

There's more than one way to skin a cat.

Externally, she and the new guy kept a polite façade. She was here to protect Navarre. He was doing the same for Tamaz and Erckens. All three were oblivious, drinking, toasting each other, laughing, and carrying on.

Oh, the terrible lies and stories men will tell when they're drunk.

In vino, veritas. So they say.

Only the accountant, Almássy, was relatively sober, matching the rest of the men roughly sip to bottle as they went.

"No," Captain Tamaz slurred out loudly. "I insist. You will believe me after that."

Hadiiye had no idea what the men were on about. She'd been mostly filtering out their words and watching the room. Navarre was too canny to start anything here. But suddenly everybody was in motion, sliding out of the booth towards her and standing up all wobbly.

"Come, my friend," Tamaz continued. "You will see the truth of it. They are all doomed. DOOMED!"

The drunks erupted in a symphony of cheers and giggles. It was weird, even by normal standards, if there was such a thing on a pirate space station.

You could tell a pirate by how well he walked, blind-stinking-drunk. Tamaz had the look of a man who could walk across a high-wire between buildings in a cross wind, right now. Everything seemed to be battened down perfectly water-tight as he strode down the stairs, glancing over his shoulder at the rest of the group as he went.

Javier was much more fluid and relaxed as he moved. Hadiiye chalked that up to all the food they had eaten earlier. She wondered if the others would realize how sober he was.

Hadiiye made eye contact with the burly bouncer and indicated silently that he should be up front and she would be at the back. He thought about it for a moment, shrugged, and got moving. There wasn't really a good choice at this point. She was obviously a stranger, so would encounter friction at every waypoint, while he could ease them through. She was just along for the ride.

Now she just needed to figure out where they were going to take her.

PART THREE

DEEP INSIDE, where nobody could see, Javier smiled.

Captain Navarre was a happy, cheerful drunk, making toasts, telling jokes, and egging the other men on, like any best buds freshly-met in a bar. Life was always a party.

But let's face it. Until you wake up three days later, in different county, wearing someone else's pants, you're bush league. Bonus points if you have a Shore Patrol hat on at the time.

It was a shame he never got to keep those hats. It would have been an awesome collection, all things considered.

But he was here to do a job. An ugly, ill-conceived thing, but one he was perfectly suited for. After all, it just might involve that crazy Amazon bitch ending up dead, and not be his fault.

How much better could it get?

"But how did you manage to keep her quiet?" Navarre asked. Well, slurred. It was a wet, messy sound, but all drunks have that same sloppy accent when two and a half sheets to the wind. It might be Shakespeare to them.

"Bah, she is pussycat," Tamaz roared back, slamming back another shot of something pink and then hammering down his shatter-proof shot glass. "And I use her to kill rest of them."

"Really, Abraam," Navarre replied with the utter seriousness only a drunk can manage. "A pussycat?"

"Come, my friend," Tamaz continued. "You will see truth of it. They are all doomed. DOOMED!"

Navarre nodded. As Tamaz started to move.

It made perfect sense. Tamaz wanted to go walksies. We shall go walksies.

All three drunks made it vertical. The accountant was there. Killer-babe was there.

And who are you?

Navarre was looking at someone new, from about the center of the other guy's chest. Definitely a him. Pecs but no boobs.

He leaned back, craning to see the man's face, all the way up there, and nearly toppled over backwards. A hand, a gigantic paw really, slashed out and caught him easily by the front of his doublet, held him effortlessly, tugged him carefully upright.

Navarre stepped back and executed a perfect Court bow. Deportment classes had not been a waste. He could do this even dead drunk.

Or faking dead drunk, as he was now.

In the middle of his motion, obscured by moving parts and backs of heads, Navarre clicked a small button hidden inside his belt buckle. Javier smiled.

One silent Ping for mankind.

"Thank you, good sir," he slurred, rather louder than required, and then staggered after Tamaz and Erckens.

Damn. That guy was big. And fast. And looked smart, too. Good thing this was only the scouting portion of the trip. Probably need some heavy artillery to take him down. Or just blow the whole damned section open to vacuum. Make the dude a space dragon or something.

Right now, Navarre and Javier were both just looking forward to seeing Sykora again.

THE FEET KNEW THE WAY, having navigated it enough times that the mind could focus elsewhere. Abraam Tamaz felt the joy of absolute power wash over him as he went to visit his love, waiting for him like a songbird in a gilded cage.

And traps, traps within traps. Doom within spirals of destruction.

Tamaz did not trust this Captain Navarre fellow. The timing was too close. A helpful stranger arrives just as his grand trap for Sokolov was about to slam shut?

What were the odds that the fates were conspiring so brightly on his side? They had never loved him so much before today.

Thus, traps within traps.

Tamaz smiled up at Morghan, his own personal Kodiak bear, as they passed through another set of hatches, closing on the edge of the station. He could be as drunk and relaxed as he wanted with that man about. Utter loyalty. Unbelievable ferocity. Absolute sobriety. Navarre might have brought along a killer, the woman had that look about her, but nothing could stand against Morghan.

Around a long hallway, ever-so-slightly curved, the ship's main personnel hatch came into view, carefully guarded by two of his crew. Tamaz smiled to himself.

That was power. Right there. Crew on duty instead of drunk off their asses like their captain.

Tamaz stepped to one side and gestured his new friend to precede him.

"I give you, the starship *Salekhard*," he said grandly, knowing the title would be lost on them.

After all, how many people would recognize the name of an Imperial Russian prison camp for exiles in the far wilds of Homeworld Siberia? Or guess how appropriate it might be…

In through the double airlocks and onto his ship. Tamaz found himself jostling up against the woman Navarre had brought, as they waited for the airlock doors to cycle. He resisted the urge to reach out and caress one of her breasts.

They were quite lovely.

He was the captain, it was his ship. But it would be rude. Especially if Navarre might truly be a possible ally against Sokolov, and not a plant or a spy. He could always kill the man and have the woman later, if that was the necessity of things.

He settled for a deep draft of her perfume. Sykora never wore perfume. The old Sykora. Who knew what he might convince her to do, once he owned her body and soul.

Once she existed only to please him.

The thought was more intoxicating than any narcotic might dream of being.

He turned to lead them deeper into the ship, accidentally brushing against a warm, full breast as he went, supreme in all things.

HADIIYE WAS SLIGHTLY bemused at the situation. Wilhelmina wanted to gouge his eyes out. But then, Hadiiye hadn't been touched by this man or his first mate.

Rape existed on a spectrum, not a point. They had stayed generally at the emotional end, with enough groping to make their point, without ever getting truly physical.

Wilhelmina the psychologist wondered if either Tamaz or Erckens even really liked women, or needed frightened little girls or boys to get excited. Certainly, they hadn't gotten aroused by the situation, but rape was a crime of power, not passion.

Wilhelmina had simply not let them have power over her.

Hadiiye was willing to geld them with a dull spoon for her anyway. It would be an improvement to the species, to keep them from propagating.

Especially when Tamaz got that look in his eye.

One of his hands twitched, like it was going to go up her skirt. Hadiiye might even let it be, considering the situation, the location, the company.

Or she might pull a shiv and touch his cheek, right below the eyeball, just to get his attention. She didn't owe any man anything. Except pain and a slow, lingering death.

She smiled at Tamaz as he changed his mind. She even suffered the space violation with a light smile as he leaned forward and inhaled her scent. The way his eyes rolled back, half-closed, was fascinating.

He certainly wasn't thinking about her.

Food for thought.

Salekhard proved to be a medium freighter as they tromped her decks. It was built more durable than hulls from her time, but five centuries of technology and metallurgy will do that.

There was far more crew than a freighter this size would normally carry, but she was expecting that. This was a pirate, after all. Play possum until someone got close, and then turn into wolf in sheep's clothing.

From her recent studies, improvements in jump drives and life support systems meant that a crew of twenty to thirty would be normal on a vessel of this scale. She had probably already seen twice that count, just crossing half the linear distance and going up three decks.

They certainly weren't going to shoot their way in, if they wanted to rescue Djamila. Hadiiye was patient. Navarre would have a plan.

The party came to rest at a closed hatch. It was like that moment when the tide turned, pooling all the water to stillness in a bay, just before it started to run back out. She missed the smell of Dundee.

Tamaz gifted them with his warm, drunk smile, a canary in his mouth, at least metaphorically.

"And now, my friends," he said, summoning his best diction from the depths of his drunkenness. "Now, you will see the power that I wield. The glory. I give you, the dragoon, Sykora."

He turned and theatrically pushed the button to slide the hatch into the wall.

Hadiiye was last into the small room, crowded with five other bodies around the table.

No, six. Strange little man tucked into a corner, crowded back from the killers around him as if they had a sour smell. She sniffed. Nothing but the musk of big men and her perfume.

Probably not something that turned the little man on, either way.

They jostled around, finding a calm point. Again, tides swirling, eddying.

In her heels, Hadiiye was taller than anyone in the room but the big guy, so she could see over shoulders and didn't need to press forward.

Hadiiye suppressed any gasp, any emotional response, any clue that might suggest she was more or less than she seemed. They had arrived at a moment of life or death.

Djamila.

The dragoon was tied naked to a modified hospital gurney. Trussed, really. Immobilized by someone who was extremely serious about his business and not just exploring his kinbaku kinks on a long woman.

And wires everywhere. Every good nerve cluster appeared to be getting a jolt of electricity, except the one between her legs.

So, pain, but at no point pleasure. About what she expected from these men. Brutality, with no understanding of what made a woman tick. Especially not one like Djamila.

Morons.

Not that she would help correct their misunderstandings, but it was certainly ammunition for what she had planned for them.

Lit cigarettes and bolt cutters came to mind.

Hadiiye stepped back. She had seen what she needed. Her job was to bodyguard Navarre and keep him safe, especially here in the pits of hell.

Navarre stepped close to Djamila, leaned over, got very, very still. He could probably smell her sweat from there.

"You see, Captain Navarre," Tamaz gloated. "I have succeeded where all others have failed. The woman is mine."

She watched Navarre's head turn to look at Tamaz, his face unreadable but closed.

"Would you like to say hello to her?" Tamaz asked innocently.

Hadiiye felt the room around her grow cold. She suddenly understood why Tamaz had been so easy about inviting them into his lair to see his prize.

It was a trap.

Masterful, really. Bring them here where they couldn't escape. Bring Djamila out of her tortured state, present the strangers, see her response before she could collect herself.

Navarre, they would kill out of hand. There was a very good chance Wilhelmina would end up on a table just like this one, if something went wrong.

Her death might linger over years.

There was nothing of Javier in the man before her. Captain Navarre was supreme, regal. He was vengeance, personified. He had a voice that could etch metal.

"That would be lovely," Navarre drawled, acid dripping on every word.

The other men had grown suddenly tense, respecting the possibility of violence on close quarters. Very few people would make it out of a room like this alive, most likely, if something bad happened.

Navarre stood perfectly still. Calm, poised, almost happy. She watched him look down at Djamila again, smile with the warmth of an owl sneaking up on a field mouse.

"Please?" he continued, putting true emotion into his voice as he looked at Tamaz.

Captain Tamaz nodded to the weird, little dumpy man in the corner, who leapt forward and began jiggering with a machine by Djamila's head. Hadiiye has taken it for a bio-monitor at first glance.

It was apparently the source of Djamila's pain.

She watched Djamila's body grow limp and relaxed as the electricity subsided.

Tamaz worked his way around to the other side of the table with the doctor, leaving him a clear view of Navarre's reaction.

And, coincidentally, moving him out of the way if Erckens and the giant needed to get physical in a small volume. Hadiiye let herself fade back just a bit more, and turned slightly to the side, in case she needed to get at a hidden knife quickly. Not that it would probably matter, but anything in a maelstrom.

Even from here, the smell of whatever they put under Djamila's nose was putrid. Almost raw ammonia. Certainly, it got through.

Djamila opened her eyes slowly. She came to herself and looked up at Javier/Navarre, leaning over her, leering.

"Hello, princess," Captain Navarre said cheerfully.

The big guy tensed. Erckens tensed. Hell, all of them puckered up a little.

Djamila, bless her soul, actually growled up at Javier, around the gag in her mouth.

Navarre was looking away from her, at Tamaz, when he straightened up, so Hadiiye couldn't see his face. But the emotion in his stance, his body language, was pure triumph.

"Whatever you have planned for her and Sokolov," Navarre purred loudly. "I'm in."

Wilhelmina reconsidered whether bringing Javier here had been a good idea, after all.

PART FOUR

The bed was cold.

Not physically. Wilhelmina had thrown the covers down to keep from completely overheating as Javier slept. The man was a portable furnace.

No, emotionally.

The need for Navarre and Hadiiye to remain in character all the long way back to their own ship, having seen what they needed to see and made friends enough with Captain Tamaz.

Navarre silent in thought and triumph. Hadiiye silent in worried fear.

There was no love lost between Javier and Djamila. She knew that. She had hoped that his own decency would overcome his hatred, at least long enough to save Sykora from a fate worse than death.

She was beginning to question that assumption.

Javier barely snored as he slept beside her.

There had been little physicality between them, save the one time. It was normally almost like sleeping in a bed with her brother, when they were still children.

Tonight, it was like sleeping with a soon-to-be ex-husband, trapped in a bed and unable to go sleep on a non-existent couch.

The ship was too small to get away from him.

Had she really brought them all this distance, just so he could get his revenge on Sykora personally?

The thought sent shivers down her spine, in spite of herself, or Djamila's stories, or that look in Javier's eyes.

And that vial. Tamaz's frumpy little assistant had pulled the glass tube, filled with a bright green liquid, from a nearby refrigerator, for Tamaz to show off to his new, drunken friends.

Wilhelmina had studied the social sciences, the liberal arts. She had degrees in sociology, psychology, history, and accounting. She barely knew anything about medicine, beyond the basics of field first aid on primitive planets.

The conversation between Tamaz and Navarre had quickly gone over her head. But that was to be expected from someone who once owned a steel coffee mug with *THE SCIENCE OFFICER* etched into the side. It had made good memento. Wilhelmina wondered if it would be a terrible reminder if they failed.

Tamaz's plan was simple.

Empty the vial into Sykora with a needle.

Ransom her off to Sokolov as a carrier.

Wait twenty-four hours for a plague to vector its way through *Storm Gauntlet*'s crew.

Death. For everyone but Djamila.

Tamaz and his friends had already deserved whatever punishment could be meted out. Now they deserved a first class trip to hell.

Hadiiye looked forward to punching their tickets.

Javier stirred.

A hand snaked out under the sheets, caught hers before she could twitch it away.

She was trapped.

He opened his eyes.

Javier, not Navarre.

"Are you ready to talk?" he asked her simply.

"Do you have anything to say that I'll want to hear?" she replied with far more edge that she had expected when she opened her mouth.

He stared at her for several seconds.

"Djamila Sykora is almost everything I hate about deep space," Javier began with a shrug. "Stick-up-her-butt rules-follower who is constantly belittling everyone around her for not measuring up to the impossible standards she sets."

Wilhelmina nodded, unwilling to trust her reply.

"But she's just an asshole," Javier said. "Tamaz and his friends are *evil*."

Something changed in his face. In his hand as well, pressed up against her side and twined with her own.

"Once upon a time," he continued. "I was one of the good guys. It didn't work out, for reasons we won't go into here. But nobody deserves that."

What *THAT* was, she left dangling, just as he did. This was yet another side of an already complicated man, one she had certainly never met before.

Wilhelmina wondered again if she had ever met the real Javier Aritza, or just the many roles he played to keep the world at bay. She could tell that there was someone underneath that façade but there were enough flashes to keep her guessing.

She felt his hand give hers a squeeze.

"I'm not doing this for her, `Mina," he said simply. "I'm not doing it for you. I'm doing it because it's right."

Oh.

She wondered about future conversations she might have with this man about the nature of evil.

What was *evil?*

Javier Aritza did not frequently strike her as an especially deep philosopher. Certainly not a pre-eminent existentialist.

And yet.

He was willing to simply step past all of his hatred for Djamila, and do the right thing, because Wilhelmina Teague had asked.

Because she needed paladins.

"So what do we do now, Javier?"

Instead of answering, he let go of her hand and rolled out of bed. She watched his butt in those old sweats as he took two steps to the piloting station and pressed a button.

"Curveball, this is Mother Hen," he said into the radio. "What is your status?"

"Primary scouting complete, Mother Hen," Suvi replied instantly. "Transmitting now."

The console chirped as a file arrived. Javier sat down to read it.

In spite of the cooler air in the room, Wilhelmina climbed out of bed and looked over Javier's shoulder as he quickly digested the document.

He looked up with a sardonic smile.

"This would be easier to do if you were wearing any clothes, 'Mina," he observed tartly. "Men do find your breasts distracting."

She considered responses for a moment with a sly smile.

This Javier was much closer to the man she had been expecting, a week ago. Nicer. Friendlier. Softer.

Navarre might prove to be an interesting lay, but he wouldn't be nearly as much fun in bed as Javier.

"So I can't tempt you?" she replied teasingly.

"You're already tempting me, woman," he said. "But

time's tight if you want to do this. I can always have you for dessert, afterwards."

Wilhelmina blushed, smiled, and turned to look for a shirt.

That would be a promise to keep him on track. She could always threaten to withhold marital favors if he got them all killed.

Hopefully that would be something to bring Javier back to her.

BOOK EIGHT: PALADIN

PART ONE

T HE STARS around her were wonderful. Suvi was home
again, however temporarily, as the little flitter silently cruised
through deep space outside the station, working hard to
sneak up on the pirate freighter, *Salekhard*, with Javier and
Dr. Teague in tow in suits.

Suvi considered Javier's plan with mixed feelings.

When she was *Mielikki*, this trick would have never
worked on her. But then, in those days she'd also been a
small warship, built to *Concord* Fleet standards and expected
to operate like an officer and a gentlewoman. She'd been
literally wired into every hatch, every vent, every everything
on her former ship.

Salekhard was just an old tired freighter. At least she
looked that way to someone looking in from the outside.
Probably the big, bad wolf if you got too close. Q-ship.

But that was the mean people aboard. *Salekhard* was just
an old iron ship. No brains, no personality. No AI cousin
aboard.

That was probably for the best, considering *Salekhard* was

in service to evil. Suvi wouldn't have to figure out a way to kill her. Javier could do this thing and they'd be off.

Suvi wished she could talk to Javier and Wilhelmina right now, but his orders had been extremely specific. No radio transmissions until he said otherwise, when they made it to the other side. Suvi looked around at the deep black of empty space instead.

Not being a starship anymore had always been painful, but now it hurt doubly so. She was back in deep space, pulling what Javier called a second-story-maneuver.

A length of line connected her to Javier and then to Wilhelmina, floating silently behind her on a tether like strange little balloons in their space-suits. He could communicate with her via hand signals, if he had anything useful to say, but right now, it was just silence.

Oh, sure. Traffic all around them. A place like *Meehu Platform* was never quiet. There were ships coming and going every hour of every day, sometimes stacked up three deep in nearby orbit awaiting a docking bay.

The comm was never quiet either, but Javier wanted them to think like cat burglars, and he didn't want any transmissions close to *Salekhard* to possibly warn anyone what they were up to.

Seriously, Javier. Who's going to see this coming?

But she kept her own counsel. Suvi'd been an officer and a gentlewoman, a scout, a pilot, a warrior. She'd never been a thief.

It was kinda cool.

She gave a little burst of power. Not much. Mostly to redirect herself down and sideways, just enough to tug Javier and Wilhelmina into line with the secondary engineering airlock she had picked out two hours ago.

A game of galactic billiards.

Contact imminent.

Suvi flared her lifters just enough to counter the mass of the two humans behind her. Bring them in to almost a dead stop relative.

It was all in the English you put on that ball, folks.

Javier landed like a cat. Wilhelmina was…

Oh, crap.

Has this woman never done an EVA? That looked like a gymnast in gravity.

Oh, right. Human reflexes. This was something you trained for. Nobody was born with it.

Well, Dragoon Sykora might have been, but that just proved the rule. That woman was scary good.

Radio? No. He'd been specific.

And he can't reach her.

And I'm out of position.

And…Hey, what are you doing, Javier? That's my tether line. Stop pulling me closer, I need to go get Wilhelmina and bring her back.

Suvi let her lifters go slack before she pulled him off the hull as well. He had magnets, but they were for walking, not holding them both down if she red-lined things. The last thing she needed was both of them floating loose out here, where someone might look out a porthole and raise an alarm, even in dock.

She waited while Javier grabbed her body with both hands, tied the line to his belt, and then pushed her softly at Wilhelmina. She felt like a game-winning free-throw, spinning slowly backwards.

Nothing but net.

It's a damned good thing I don't get airsick, bucko, or I'd have to blow electronic chunks all over you.

And worse, Javier missed.

She was going to fly right by Wilhelmina, about a half meter out of reach.

Now what do we do?

Javier tugged on the rope and snapped his arm to one side.

Great, now sideways torque as well? Are you trying to make me heave here?

And then it dawned on her. As the whip snapped her to one side and around Wilhelmina's back.

And I'm wrapped around her like a lasso.

Oh.

Right.

Maybe he *has* done this before.

I'm going to sit here very quietly and pretend like I planned it that way.

Perfect.

THE AIRLOCK DOOR slid open with a minimum of noise. Javier preferred it that way.

In dock, he knew engineering would generally be on minimum shifts with everything powered down. Unless they were rebuilding something big, in which case it would be wall to wall people and noise and he'd be caught in about two minutes.

Darkness.

Well, dimness.

Engines shut down. Jump drives off. Auxiliary power reactors on baseline. Life support dialed down as the ship drew fresh air off the station. At least, fresher air.

Stinky with a different set of trace volatile organics, at a minimum.

Salekhard was a freighter. She wasn't flashy. She certainly wasn't fast. Victims came to her.

From the drunken conversation with Tamaz, the ship

had lost a pair of cargo holds during the massive up-gunning refit that turned her into a Q-ship. Space lost had been turned into banks of generators and batteries. The center of gravity of the engineering crew had shifted well forward when that happened.

Engineering was a ghost town.

Javier grinned.

Starships in space were never shut down, but humans were humans. You set your bio-rhythms a particular way and left them there. Eight hours of duty in a twenty-four hour shift. Couple three hours for food. Couple hours personal recreation. Time for training and school recerts. Eight hours down to sleep.

Even in station, you'll keep to that pattern, with time thrown in for parties and business.

For *Salekhard*, it was the middle of the night.

The perfect time to break in.

She wasn't a navy ship, with snappy, matching uniforms for everyone, color-coded by department and rank. Tamaz might be a sociopath, but he wasn't ex-fleet.

Crew tended to either wear what they came with, or what they picked up at stations like this. In between, they would have the sorts of pants and tunic the quartermaster could sell you cheap. At that point, the only real difference between ships in space was color, because a cheap acquisitions officer was going to buy a block of sizes of everything in a single color.

On *Salekhard*, that was brown. Boring, mud-colored brown.

Fortunately, this was *Meehu Platform*. Everything was available for a price, including boring, mud-brown disguises.

Suvi went into the vast space first, quietly pinging all of engineering to map it.

Nothing.

Lights dialed down to reduce power load and save money in dock. Critical systems well lit, but the rest shadowed. Standard operating procedure.

Javier followed, mud-brown with a gym bag in one hand. Wilhelmina came last, still wearing those damned high-heeled purple combat boots under her pants.

For a moment, the evil conscience on his left shoulder suggested she should wear them to bed sometime. Nothing else, just the boots. Even the good conscience got a goofy smile on his face at that image.

Javier had Suvi's flight controller remote, hanging like a satchel to one side, just in case, but she was flying the remote. Some of his buttons apparently made happy sounds play in her cockpit, or little unicorns and toy dinosaurs race across the console. He certainly wasn't flying the craft.

"Suvi," he whispered, just loud enough for her to pick up. "Find me the entry hatch off the top-most catwalk gangway."

Instead of answering, she bounced straight up, almost silently.

Javier was reduced to sneaking over to a set of stairs and mounting them. He wasn't as quiet, but he didn't need silence. Around him, *Salekhard* groaned and creaked as systems came on and off, generators, air, and cooling systems answering the call for power or going back to sleep.

Space was only silent on the outside. On the inside, it never shut up.

Engineering had three decks of verticality. Mostly, that was the thrusters. *Salekhard* could hold a lot of mass, so the ship needed a tremendous amount of initial thrust to push it along. Doubly so when climbing out of the local gravity well to reach a safe jump range.

That just meant the rear third of the ship bulged

strangely. And you were a ways off the deck plates when looking down from that second catwalk.

Javier looked at the hatch Suvi'd found.

At least freighters followed a simple naval architecture. Either you had one main arterial corridor down the spine, with the cargo holds hanging to either side off that like ribs, or two corridors down the outsides, with individual cargo holds on the centerline.

Salekhard had central holds. That also served to mentally divide the ship into thirds. Either you were forward, with the important people close to the bridge, or aft with the engineers. Stevedores got stuck in the middle. And ignored.

It was the dead of night. In a hallway as far from the important parts of the freighter as they could get. Javier didn't really feel safe, but he figured the odds were in his favor.

"I lead," he said quietly before opening the hatch. "'Mina second. Suvi, try to stay back a little farther as an ace in the hole."

Wilhelmina nodded. Suvi flashed her running lights on and off. Javier took a deep breath and palmed the button.

The hatch opened slowly.

Nobody.

He blew out the breath and started walking. Behind him, utter silence so intense he had to turn and look back to make sure both women were still behind him.

Okay, good.

He didn't bother with a weapon. He wasn't that good to begin with, and a firefight here would screw everything quickly. Plus, both girls could take care of themselves. And hopefully him.

Instead, he was the pathfinder today. He might have had a lot to drink, but seriously, that was nothing.

Hell, the other two men might still be in bed for a number of hours, trying to recover.

Amateurs.

Javier counted his steps. Internal passageways on a ship like this didn't have happy little colored lines for tourists to follow. But there were only so many ways to build a vessel.

He turned to port and went down a side hall that wrapped around the front of engineering's bulge.

No fancy castings or curves. Just basic cubes welded together at a mostly-automated ship yard, knocking out parts twenty-four-seven and then assembling them like three dimensional jigsaw puzzles later. Corridor, cargo hold, cabin, suite. Weld A to B. Repeat with C.

Javier let his monkey brain drive. Overthinking was bad here.

If he was right, the correct hatch was about here.

Javier looked around.

Yup. That stain on the wall. The one shaped like the Blessed Madonna. The one that looked like a pulse-pistol burn scar. This was the place.

He signaled to the girls to get close, unsure if opening this hatch would trigger an alarm somewhere other than in his head.

Certainly, the clock would start running.

He reached out and pushed the button.

PART TWO

The pain ebbed.

Djamila felt the barriers around her soul coming down. The physical world grew close.

Tamaz must want to torture her again.

Certainly, the last time had been the most intense. Djamila was beginning to wonder if her sanity was finally breaking. She had actually imagined Aritza here, helping Tamaz break her.

If she was going insane, that would be the shape hell took when she got there.

That smell brought her back the rest of the way. By now, it was beginning to be impressed on her nervous system as *home*. Djamila wondered if she would carry that association to her grave.

Her eyes opened to painfully bright light. She could focus. Something was wrong.

She could move.

Tamaz was standing over her, leering at her, lusting after her, even after all these years. The first mate was with him, standing back and to one side.

115

She would have only one chance at this.

Djamila exploded off the gurney in a flash of movement, trusting her instincts to guide her.

She grabbed Tamaz by the front of his shirt and slammed him backwards into the bulkhead hard.

Djamila had no expectation she would get out of this room alive. She just wanted company on the trip to hell.

Abraam Tamaz would be a fine companion.

He didn't struggle as much as she expected him to. He barely resisted as she got her hands around his throat, lifted him bodily, and began to crush.

It would be good to kill this man.

Why wasn't he fighting? Had she knocked him out against the bulkhead?

No, his eyes were open, boring into hers from so close.

And why wasn't the first mate trying to stop her? All she really wanted right now was to die in battle.

Was that too much to ask?

Pain. There. Yes. Good. I'm alive enough to feel pain. This isn't a torture-induced fantasy overtaking my sanity. This is someone pinching my earlobe hard enough to hurt. Not pulling, just pinching.

What?

"Djamila," Wilhelmina Teague's voice penetrated her haze. "I need you to listen to me. Please come back to me."

Come back? Where else would I be?

No, better. Why would Wilhelmina Teague be here in my illusion? She doesn't deserve to die with me. Perhaps to have vengeance, though. That would make sense.

The pain became a pull. Djamila felt her head turn, being turned, being drug around to one side. Someone was there.

It wasn't Aaron Erckens, after all. It was a woman. A very tall woman. A familiar looking woman.

"Djamila Sykora," the stranger said. "Please listen to me. Please hear me. Please come back to the present."

The present? The present was a torture chamber on Abraam Tamaz's ship, slowing losing her sanity rather than finally give her soul to that man. It was impending death, perhaps taking Zakhar down with her, because she was too stubborn to simply allow herself to die on this table.

She would make them kill her. Right here. Right now. It would be a good death.

But that face looked familiar.

I've seen you somewhere before.

And then the woman leaned close and kissed her lightly on the lips.

What?

The shock broke through the final haze around Djamila's brain.

"Wilhelmina?" she asked, slamming suddenly back into the present.

But if that's Wilhelmina, then who am I choking?

Djamila turned her head back as the pull on her earlobe lessened.

Aritza.

Briefly, she considered finishing the job. It wouldn't take much. A little twist, some lateral torque. A quick and painless death.

Aritza deserved it.

And yet, he had saved her life. More than once.

And he wouldn't be here without Sokolov's permission. That mean was Zakhar coming soon.

The Captain should have been the one to awaken her, if he was here. Aritza was standing in.

Djamila let Aritza's feet touch the deck again.

"Hello, Princess," he said again. "Maybe I should have wakened you with a kiss?"

Djamila nearly killed him anyway for that. Wilhelmina pulled her ear sideways as she started to.

Djamila let her head come around. Aritza could always suffer a tragic accident later.

Wilhelmina handed her a bundle of clothes and a black wig.

"Put this on," she said.

Djamila let the moment direct her. She wasn't up for more than pure reaction at this point. Obviously, they had a plan.

Djamila realized she was still nude. There was a towel in the bundle. She used it briefly to dry herself.

Aritza was busy ogling her as she did.

You're just as bad as they are, bastard.

She dressed quickly. Brown pants. White t-shirt. Brown tunic. Her own ship slippers from *Storm Gauntlet*, the ones custom made for her long skinny feet.

"Are you you yet?" Aritza asked simply.

Djamila considered the answer. She had been in another world for some time. Days, possibly weeks if he was here now. Her survival had required retreating into the unpassable mountains in her mind and waiting out the winter.

Her rescue force had arrived with spring. They wanted to know if she could handle herself.

If she could fight.

Djamila felt a snarl take hold of her face.

She wasn't dead yet. Of course she could still fight.

She nodded at him professionally, unwilling to trust her tongue just yet.

He smiled. And surprised the hell out of her.

"Here," he said.

Djamila was suddenly holding a late-model pulse pistol in one hand.

Automatically, she confirmed the safety, the power pack, the grip, the sights.

"Now what?" she asked him.

Aritza had obviously planned this. Let his plan run forward until she understood it enough to improve it. He was a science officer, not a killer.

Not like her.

"Now we escape," Wilhelmina answered.

"Not quite yet," Aritza said.

Djamila watched him walk to a small refrigerator unit in a corner and squat down. She did not understand the vial of greenish liquid he pulled out, but Wilhelmina's gasp of shock told her many things.

"First, I owe that man something."

The harsh look on Aritza's face matched the feral anger burning deep in her soul. Perhaps he was a killer, after all.

PART THREE

Hᴀᴅɪɪʏᴇ ʜᴀᴅ to explain it to Wilhelmina. Hadiiye already grasped the fundamental point Navarre was making. Wilhelmina was aghast at the possibilities.

Navarre was a hard man. She knew that. She had seen it first hand, along the way here.

This was something else entirely. This was verging on evil itself. This wasn't fighting fire with fire. This was burning the whole damned world down and starting over.

This was Ragnarok. Twilight of the Gods. This was Navarre as Surtur.

So, Javier was a specialist in the old Norse mythology cycles, as well?

And Hadiiye was going to help. It fell to Wilhelmina to put a stop to it.

There were some things that were simply too evil to contemplate. This was one of them.

She started to speak. Hadiiye stopped her, reminded her that they had to escape first.

Wilhelmina subsided. For now. They had a long road to

go to escape this trap. And a shipful, a stationful, a galaxyful of pirates to escape.

Still, Navarre had taken all four vials. He had the big one, plus all three of the little ones that were apparently the antidote. That had to count for something.

First they would escape *Salekhard*. Then they would discuss the ethics of biological warfare.

So far, so good.

Navarre kinked his head to one side, then the other. He opened his mouth wide enough to pop the jaw, then closed it.

There would be a couple of really good hickeys on his neck tomorrow, assuming he lived that long. But at least Hadiiye had kept the dragoon from killing him.

Today, anyway. She still had that light in her eyes, that hatred, that barely-in-control rage.

It made him warm all over.

He got a nod from both women, indicating their readiness. They both had pistols, although he had no idea how good Hadiiye might be. Sykora was the ballerina of death, so he had no worries there. Not right now.

Tomorrow? That would settle itself.

Home first.

The little flight controller came active and showed him the hallway.

Suvi was following orders and had found a quiet intersection where she could see partway back to engineering and all of this corridor. And she was at least generally listening to the joystick controls, aware of who the audience was today.

Things were still quiet. And dim.

You would think, plugged into station power, that a captain would leave the lights on full. They weren't going to cost that much, especially once your docking fees would already cover part of it.

But some people were just too cheap for their own good, always cutting corners instead of doing it right. *Storm Gauntlet* came to mind, at least when he had first boarded her, but those corners being cut had saved his life. Probably. Maybe not. Who knew where he might have ended up if they had sold him to an agricultural station as labor?

Water under a burned bridge.

Javier opened the door. Navarre would had done something grand and obnoxious here. Javier wanted to sneak out the back door just like he had come in. He had to take charge here, so they could get out alive.

Into the corridor.

Nothing.

Two killer girls steps behind him silent. Eerie.

"So glad I upgraded the auto-pilot on this thing," he stage muttered to the women as he typed.

Suvi hopped to the next intersection and looked around.

Emptiness.

Javier followed, remembering to look both ways before crossing this dangerous street.

Now they were back in the main corridor, a straight shot aft to engineering.

A nameplate on a door caught his attention.

Burakgazi.

He only knew one person with that name. A short, skinny engineer with a heart-shaped face who had gone off with Wilhelmina to keep that old ship running.

That was too much for coincidence. He pushed the button to open the hatch.

Yup. Score one for the good guys as she looked up from a bunk.

"Javier?"

"Rescue, kid," he replied. "Move."

She was up off the bed in a flash.

Javier looked around.

There. Alferdinck. Navigator-extraordinaire.

Javier pushed the button.

"Piet, let's go," he said into the opening space.

The tall Dutchman didn't ask, just moved.

Javier parked Suvi in place with a quick command and turned to the girls.

"'Mina," he said. "You lead. Take everybody to that engineering hatch but don't go through. I'll bring up the rear with better sensors, so nobody sneaks up on us. Go."

Two extremely nice bottoms flowed by him. Well, three, but Afia's wasn't even in the same league as the taller women. It wasn't the time or place to really stop and appreciate Wilhelmina or Sykora, but they were still nice. Even if he couldn't imagine two women less alike.

"What are we looking for?" Suvi typed on his read-out.

"Nothing," he typed back. "Any bad guys will be coming from the bow. The girls can handle engineers. Let's go."

Javier had gone two steps when the alarms started.

"Warning," a woman's warm voice filled the corridor. "Enemy boarding parties at large. All crew shelter in place. Security teams to red alert."

Well, crap. Still, better than he had been expecting. Probably a video monitor in a hallway somewhere, or they would have seen Sykora leave the bed. Of course, that assumed anybody but Tamaz got to watch her. That would be like him. Probably an alarm on the other two crew.

Wilhelmina and the others were outside the engineering hatch.

Wilhelmina pushed the button as he approached, but nothing happened.

"They've locked it," Sykora said harshly, obviously blaming him for everything. "Now what?"

Javier held his snarky comment inside. They would gain nothing but lost time right now.

"You remember my first remote?" he asked the dragoon, pointing at Suvi back over one shoulder.

Sykora just nodded, her eyes a little bigger than a moment ago as she realized the new one was much larger.

"You were sad it wasn't armed, as I remember," he continued. "I fixed that with this version."

"Who let you have a weapon?" she snarled quietly.

Javier pointed to the one in her hand.

"Probably the same people who wanted me to rescue you," he retorted.

She refrained from commenting. Or doing anything stupid. Probably for the best. She might be fast. Suvi would be faster. And didn't particularly like Sykora.

"Everybody step back behind me," Javier said, fiddling with buttons. "I need to pretty much overload the turret to do this."

Hopefully, the stunt pilot was listening. He didn't even have controls for that turret programmed on his console. She would have to handle everything. Besides, it was her ship now.

A bright red targeting reticule appeared on one of his screens, blinking lightly. Oh, yeah. Stunt pilot to be sure.

Javier felt like he was flying a World War One Red Baron game. It had that feel to it. Maybe that was what she'd programmed for herself.

He made a note to ask her later. She had access to most of history to look things up.

Right now, he moved the impact point up and left a little.

"Everyone close your eyes," he called over the wailing sirens.

He did the same as he pushed the button to fire.

A light strobed through his eyelids.

Javier blinked. A new message appeared on his console

Warning: onboard power at 9 percent. Please charge as soon as possible.

Nine percent? But that would mean…

Javier looked up.

He had meant to blow the locking mechanism apart, so Sykora could crank the door open manually.

Suvi had damned near blown the thing off the rails.

So much for sneaky. Everybody on the ship probably felt that one.

"Sykora leads," he said. "'Mina follows. I'm last with the remote."

Nine percent power? Wow. But that was still good enough for the rest of the day, assuming nothing bad happened from here.

Or rather, nothing Sykora couldn't handle with a pulse pistol.

Which was nothing at all.

PART FOUR

Abraam Tamaz came awake at an alarm beeping madly.

He was tired, he was groggy, he had drank way too much Sambuca last night. His head rang with the pounding of large industrial machines making fender panels again, on the inside of his skull.

It wasn't the duty alarm. That had a much different tone. And it wasn't a system alarm. They were docked to a station. What kind of emergency might strike them here?

The world did not want to come into focus.

He knew it should make sense, but the alcohol had evaporated into a lovely fog this morning, making his head feel like a field in Flanders on a quiet, fall day. Nothing but bundles and rumbles of clouds moving about.

He staggered to the console and pushed the red button to silence the alarm, mostly on auto-pilot. Two still did not want to work with two to make any number, let alone four.

The sideboard was close. Tamaz grabbed a dirty glass and poured in a dollop of bitters and a finger of rum, followed by a good zap of soda water. He swirled the mad concoction around the glass a few times to stir it, then slammed the whole thing down the back of his throat in one go, letting the fire burn all the way down and sort out the mess it found in his stomach.

That seemed to cut through the fog. He felt sunrise slowly begin to burn away the clouds that had taken root in his head.

Tamaz blinked furiously a few times, willing himself to conscious thought. It was a hard road this morning.

Why was he awake?

Thought grew slowly concrete, but he got there.

The alarm.

The laboratory.

Someone had opened the door without putting in the correct code combination. Nobody but he and Igor knew that combination. Nobody but the two of them had any reason, any business whatsoever, going in there.

Tamaz lunged suddenly at the console. He took three tries to enter his password correctly into the keypad, coming dangerously close to locking himself out and forcing him to reset the entire authentication suite from files in his personal safe.

There.

That was the alarm from the lab. Bring up the camera.

She was gone.

His love, his treasure, his little titmouse in her gilded cage. She had flown.

Someone was going to die for this.

Slowly, painfully. Someone would take years understanding the depths of his vengeance. Who?

Quickly, Tamaz cycled through cameras.

There. In the hallway. Several figures.

NAVARRE!

I would have given that man Sokolov's head on a stick as a holiday present.

It was all a sham. He was here to rescue the woman, not avenge himself on her. Not like Tamaz would do.

Frantically, he toggled the comm until he found the channel he wanted.

"Security station," he growled. "We have intruders aboard. Lock down all access ports to the station and scramble your teams. I want them alive."

Let that bastard make his way forward. Most of the crew would be at the front of the ship. And waiting.

"Acknowledged, Captain," the man replied. "Stand by."

Tamaz watched the man begin to push buttons on his own console.

Somewhere, heavily armed men were moving towards armaments lockers. Death would not be quickly coming for Navarre and his woman. Women.

Tamaz watched the group approach the starboard axial corridor on deck one. That made logical sense. It gave them access almost all the way to the bow airlocks if they moved quickly enough.

What? Why are they headed aft? What was in engineering?

Tamaz slapped his hand on another red button and held it down.

"Warning," a woman's computerized voice filled the corridor. "Enemy boarding parties at large. All crew shelter in place. Security teams to red alert."

Normally, that was recycled on a loop when they had played dead and allowed another vessel to try to take them. Wolf in sheep's clothing. Let them think the crew was in a total panic, but also it let his crew know to lock themselves away from trouble, because the hunters were armed and stalking.

Tamaz opened a secondary drawer close by and pulled out a larger pistol than he normally carried. This was a stun-only model, a neural whip designed to overload someone's brain, without actually killing them.

It would just put them down, so he could capture them for play later.

Navarre was not allowed to steal his toys. He would keep the other woman as a prize.

But they were all going to die for this.

PART FIVE

"Are you sure about this?" Javier heard one of the women yell. He wasn't paying enough attention to tell them apart right now. Around them, flashing red lights and a painfully overloaded siren wailed.

"Do you want to be here when Tamaz arrives?" he yelled back, pounding down stairs, almost flying, and letting his feet touch about one in three as he went.

Suvi cheated and dropped straight down the outside of the stairwell. She would beep if she saw anybody, but her gun was pretty much just for show at this point. Still, it had saved them a lot of time at a moment when the sands might be running out.

Sykora probably could have passed him if she'd wanted to, but she was too busy looking everywhere to move around him without falling on her face. And how Wilhelmina ran down stairs in fourteen centimeter heels was a mystery for the ages. But she did.

At least Piet and Afia kept up.

Javier hit the main deck as a hatch opened one level above them, at the far end of the open space, from the forward sections. Men poured through it. Javier didn't take time to count. It was enough.

The pirates opened fire wildly, beams ringing off stairs and rails and metal but not hitting anyone. Not yet.

Sykora was apparently in her element now. Javier was facing enough of the right direction to see her pop off three shots in rapid succession.

The first one blew up a significant chunk of railing on the catwalk, right about dead center of the guy moving behind it. He survived because the metal exploded instead. The second and third hit the two men in front of that other guy. They got drilled dead center, from fifty meters away, both shooter and target moving rapidly in three dimensions.

Seriously, that woman was scary.

Javier raced across the open space toward the open airlock hatch, three steps behind Suvi. Fire erupted behind him.

After a moment, Javier could identify when the girls were firing versus when the boys upstairs opened up. The pulse pistol had a higher pitch than the rifles the boys were toting. It took him a second to identify that sound.

Neural lash.

Crap. Someone over there was playing rough.

There was nothing like getting tagged with a beam of coherent sound designed to scramble all your brain cells. Easy way to take prisoners, especially the kind you might sell on the open market later.

Not that Javier figured Tamaz would be selling him, if it came to that.

Another round of incoming fire.

For one giddy moment, Javier considered venting all of engineering to space. It would end the threat of the neural lash, at least until someone went back for something heavier, something that would work without atmosphere. And he'd be long gone by then.

Javier made it to cover and turned back to check on everyone. Afia had apparently been in his hip pocket the whole time. She was already past him and back to the far deep end of the airlock. Piet was right behind that.

That left the girls.

They had both paused midway to provide covering fire for the rest of the crew. There were already half a dozen men down over there, but more were pouring into the room from other doors every second.

Wilhelmina moved first, apparently responding to commands from Sykora. That one was a black widow spider. 'Mina's movement drew several men from cover to take a shot.

Sykora got most of them.

Did that woman actively worship Death, or something? Were these human sacrifices to appease her harsh mistress? How could anybody be that good?

Sykora was off like a jack-rabbit as everybody over there ducked, perhaps cowed into submission by the havoc she had just wrought. The body count was certainly impressive.

Javier watched her move. The ballerina of death.

Slow-motion.

She had a smile on her face that looked almost orgasmic for a moment.

Someone got lucky.

Sykora's hair haloed around her head as a beam found her.

Her face screwed up in pain, slackened into nothingness.

She toppled, fell, slid, halted.

Javier was off without hesitation.

"Cover me," he yelled frantically at Wilhelmina as he ran past her into the valley of death.

There was no time for thought, just action.

Zig.

Fade.

Beams.

Drift.

Race.

Javier slid into home with the game-winning run, grabbing Sykora's pistol and firing three shots randomly before stuffing into a pocket as he grabbed Sykora's belt and used her mass to anchor him in his slide.

Somewhere, Wilhelmina was pouring fire back up-range at the bad guys. Nothing fancy, just keep them ducked.

No time to think. No time to breathe.

Javier hoisted the massive woman up into a fireman's carry and staggered to one side, fueled by adrenaline and fear. Tamaz would not be a pleasant captor. Not like Zakhar. Not even like Sykora.

Somehow, he made it to the airlock.

Wilhelmina went to close the airlock hatch, but he grabbed her hand before she did.

"Keep firing," he said.

'Mina nodded and leaned out, randomly potting panels and catwalks as quickly as she could pull the trigger. The charge pack wouldn't last very long at this rate.

It didn't need to.

Javier dumped Sykora full out before him. He squatted long enough to peel an eyelid, both eyelids.

Unconscious, but not permanently scrambled. Hours recovering, instead of months.

It happened, from time to time. Instead of just fuzzing everything, the beams would hit something important and scramble it like an egg. That was like suffering a medium-sized stroke. Curable, but months in rehab learning to walk and talk again. Most unpleasant.

It was his lucky day. Or hers. If you could call it that.

Javier would have liked to take the time to put on a proper space suit on Sykora for what was coming next. This would shortly qualify in the top ten dumbest things he had ever attempted.

They'd all be dead if he took the time.

Outside, the room grew quiet.

Javier considered his options. None of them were good. Conversely, not all of them were suicidal.

"Navarre," Tamaz yelled from somewhere outside. "I'll give you credit for style and balls. You almost pulled it off. If you surrender right now, I promise to kill you and the girl quick. I know Sykora is done. Let it go."

Wilhelmina muttered a word under her breath that would have made Javier's career-navy father blush.

Javier nodded at her, with a hard smile. He reached into the bag and pulled out the vial of green liquid, weighing its immense gravity with one hand.

"What are you doing?" Wilhelmina whispered fiercely as she glanced over at him.

"It's not enough to escape them, 'Mina," he murmured back. "It's not enough to rescue everyone. He must be stopped, destroyed."

"There's no other way?" she asked.

"Do you want him to keep doing this to people like you and Sykora?"

He watched the flicker of pain cross her face. He knew there were stories untold about Tamaz. He could guess the script.

Add that to the bill.

Wilhelmina ground her teeth for a moment and closed her eyes.

Javier wondered if it was a prayer, but Hadiiye looked back out of them when they opened.

"Paladins are men and women of the sword, Javier," she said calmly.

It was almost frightening the way she could do that. But it was enough.

Javier took a second to locate his target.

There. Primary air intake vents for the life-support generator. Suck in all the bad air, pass it through a hydroponics system to feed the fish and plants, push cleaner air up into the ship. Repeat. A lovely, efficient design.

Javier took a step and snapped his arm forward, gunning for the runner coming around third in the bottom of the ninth.

His aim was perfectly timed, dead accurate. The vial impacted on the vent cover with a satisfying thump.

And fell to the deck unharmed.

Javier muttered something that might have made Wilhelmina blush. He dug for the pistol in his pocket, pulled it out, and began to sight.

"Navarre?" Tamaz called. "What's it going to be?"

Apparently, he had missed the vial flying in the dimness and haze.

Javier felt Hadiiye's hand on his before he got settled.

"Can you use that thing?" she asked.

Javier shrugged. "Probably."

"I thought so," she continued.

Javier watched her raise her own pistol in one motion and fire a single shot that dead-centered the vial. It shattered, spewing a greenish slop that was quickly sucked into the vent.

That was the lovely part of a pulse-pistol, as opposed to a disruptor. It used a force bolt instead of heat. Rupture, without the risk of cooking the green liquid and killing all the nasty bugs floating in it.

Javier watched just long enough to be sure, and then slammed the airlock door closed.

"Afia," he said, turning. "Deploy the emergency cocoon and get Sykora into it first. You and Piet next."

He turned to the control panel and emptied three shots into it in a rapture of smoke and sparks.

"What about the suits?" Wilhelmina asked.

"Can you get one on in thirty seconds?" he replied.

"Watch me," she said, pulling her tunic over her head.

Javier would have liked to watch more as her nudity unfolded, but there was no time. He stripped as well.

PART SIX

THE LITTLE RUNABOUT was quickly packed to the gills as people poured out of the airlock. Javier watched Piet and Wilhelmina carry Sykora's body to the bed and carefully lay her out.

He went straight to the flight console and brought everything live.

"How much time do we have?" Afia asked from his elbow. With him sitting and her standing, she was barely taller.

"You planning on coming back to *Meehu Platform* anytime soon?" he replied.

"Not on your life, sir."

"Me, neither."

Javier pushed a button that triggered the emergency overrides on the docking mechanism.

Every station had one. Usually, the station master would use it to push back a ship in danger of exploding, to keep it from venting nastiness into the interior and killing lots more people than just the crew.

You could set them off from inside a ship if you had to. If

you suffered an emergency. Or needed to flee and didn't mind angering the stationmaster.

Somewhere nearby, bank vault doors were slamming shut and atmosphere alarms would be going off. People were going to be pissed.

Javier was in a stolen ship, fleeing a criminal enterprise, in the middle of a running gun fight, after using biological weapons. He really didn't care if they were going to give him a parking ticket after this.

The runabout lurched harshly before the gravplates could compensate.

"Piet," he called to *Storm Gauntlet*'s navigator. "I've calculated a course. Take us out that way as fast as she'll go."

"Roger that," the man replied, flowing into the seat.

Javier watched just long enough to confirm they were in safe hands, then he went to stand next to Wilhelmina, seated next to Sykora.

"How is she?" he asked.

"Been kicked by a Missouri mule," Wilhelmina replied. "Lucky for us she's tougher than one. Groggy now. Coherent in a few hours. Should be right as rain tomorrow. Assuming we survive."

"We'll survive," he said.

Javier turned around.

"Piet, how long to max acceleration?"

"Oh," the Dutchman replied sarcastically. "I was supposed to wait for that order?"

Javier smiled back at him. "Nyet, Gospodin. All ahead everything. Full speed crazy."

Javier consulted the watch in his head.

"Where are we jumping to, anyway?" Piet asked.

"Nowhere," Javier replied. "Just running."

"Javier?"

Wilhelmina looked closely at him, one hand holding Sykora's.

"'Mina?"

"How soon until we know?"

And that was the crux of it. How soon?

"We're a speedboat. He's a jumped up freighter. Let's find out."

Javier stepped close to the console. He watched Suvi land carefully on her charging ring.

After the mad dash here across open space, he knew her batteries were almost drained. But she had also saved all their lives, doing something no mere human could pull off. Like pulling a full emergency cocoon across the space between the two ships, straight to the runabout's airlock. Faster than anybody on the freighter or the station could move to intercept them.

One step ahead.

He smiled at Suvi as the little charging blinky thing stuttered. He imagined that was Suvi smiling and winking at him. He winked back.

Javier pushed a button to open a comm channel.

Winter's mantle draped itself across his shoulders as he inhaled.

"*Salekhard*, this is Navarre," he said calmly, coldly.

"I'm going to kill you, Navarre," Tamaz replied instantly.

"First you have to catch me, you amateur punk," Navarre replied, sticking the knife in and starting to twist it. "Good luck with that."

"You cannot run anywhere that I cannot find you," Tamaz continued. "And I will never cease hunting you. You have my honor on that."

"You have no honor, Abraam Tamaz," Navarre sneered. "You are the scum crusting the bottom of the barrel, after all the rotted fish have been dumped in a back alley. Right now, everyone knows you've lost her. But then, you never could keep a woman, could you?"

Navarre closed the channel with a vicious push. Virtual buttons lacked that hard tactile feedback that would have been nice now. He wished he could slam down a phone receiver, like the old movies did.

It would be more satisfying that way.

He turned to survey the crew around him. And nearly suffered the shock of his life.

Piet was watching him with a jaw dropped open. Afia's eyes were huge. Even Hadiiye was shocked.

"Piet," he growled, trying to glaze over the gap between himself and the rest. "How long until we reach those coordinates, if we don't slow down?"

The navigator just stared at him.

"Piet," he snapped his fingers. "Wake up."

"Right," the man said, tearing his eyes around to the console.

Moments passed.

"Assuming we just blow right by it," he said after a space. "A little less than two hours. Five if you want to slow down and park there. What is it?"

"A hole in space, Alferdinck," Navarre replied.

He wanted to be Javier right now. He really did.

That wasn't possible. Not today.

Today, he could only be Captain Navarre. Killer. Pirate bad-ass extraordinaire. That would have to do.

Right now, he was the captain of this little runabout. The way the rest looked at him right now left no doubt.

Time to make the best of it.

"Afia," he said, turning the vitriol in his voice down to normal conversation levels. "Could you take charge of making us some coffee? There's time before the next act."

"Coming up, sir," she said quietly.

It would be good coffee. Afia liked it dark, the same he did, especially on a day like this. The others could add cream or something to cut the bitterness down to levels tolerable for mere mortals. He wanted something monumental. This was a day for grand gestures.

Like stealing a prisoner out from under Tamaz's thumb.

Le Beau Geste.

"Contact," Piet said suddenly as a chime sounded on the console. "Looks like *Salekhard* has finally managed to detach from the station and is slowly accelerating out after us. He has weapon's lock, but won't be in range anytime soon."

"He had to behave," Navarre responded. "We could leave the place like bank robbers."

"Not complaining, sir," Piet replied. "Way happier here than there. I've got sensors and comm covered for now."

Navarre was pretty sure that this might be the most words the normally-quiet Piet Alferdinck had ever spoken to him in one setting.

"Tamaz saying anything interesting?" Navarre asked quietly.

The mad energy was beginning to ebb. The tide of the day had pooled, turned, threatened to run out of the harbor dragging him with it.

"Not unless you want to learn to curse in a few new languages, sir."

Sir? Yeah, I suppose I did just become a sir to them. I've gone from a slave on their ship to an officer in charge of things, responsible for their lives, to breaking them out of jail and rescuing them from a date with the hangman.

When the hell had he turned into one of them?

Navarre's eyes caught Djamila Sykora on the bed. Wilhelmina had covered her with a light blanket. He could see her closed eyes going back and forth, trapped in some nightmare from which she would awake to find she had traded her fate with Tamaz to a new fate with him.

I wonder which one would be worse, from her point of view?

Still, he was one of them. He was in charge. He would captain this mess to the bitter end.

Now it remained to see if he was Bligh or Christian.

Navarre reached down and activated the comm. He made sure it was a standard navigation channel this time, so everyone in the system might listen in.

"*Salekhard*," he growled. "I'm still waiting to dance. Or are too big of a coward to even come out to fight me, Tamaz?"

Across space, Tamaz gasped with rage, and then continued his stream of never-ending invective.

Navarre quickly grew bored. Javier would have at least been impressed that the pirate could go that many words between repetitions. There was a skill to that.

Tamaz was still an ass.

Navarre shut off the comm for now. It served no purpose now but to goad the man on further.

He had probably done enough already. If not, it would be there waiting.

Afia served him a mug of coffee.

"So where's the rabbit?" she asked innocently.

"Rabbit?" Navarre blinked down at the tiny woman.

"I've played too much poker with you, sir," she said. "You aren't bluffing here. So you have a rabbit you're going to pull out of a hat soon."

Navarre smiled cruelly at her, let it warm some.

"You saw that vial of liquid, Afia?" he asked conversationally. "I don't suppose you saw where I threw it?"

"No, sir," she replied firmly. "I was busy helping load the dragoon so we could abandon ship. What was it? I saw green."

Wilhelmina rose from the bed to join the conversation. She looked tired.

"It was a biological agent, Afia," she said. "Captain Tamaz was going to infect Djamila with it and then send her back to *Storm Gauntlet* to infect the rest of the crew and kill them."

The woman's dark eyes got large. "Seriously? Plague?"

"Correct," Navarre said. "Plague. We ruptured the liquid into the air intakes for *Salekhard*'s life support blowers."

Afia Burakgazi was an engineer by trade, an expert in the care and feeding of complicated mechanical systems. Navarre watched her eyes flicker back and forth as she traced the equivalent systems on *Storm Gauntlet*. Their Strike Corvette home was a purpose-built warship, instead of an up-gunned freighter, but the equations were similar.

"Biological weapon," she muttered. "Vaporize it into the wet air off hydroponics, feed it with all the right nutrients, blast it all over the ship. Infect everyone in under an hour unless they shut the whole system down."

"They can't shut the life-support systems down."

Her normally dark skin paled as she stared mutely at him.

"How do you know?"

Navarre felt a cruel smile overtake him.

"They could have, but that would have required them to vent everything and pipe in clean air from the station. And we know they didn't do that…"

"Because they detached from the station and are chasing us," Afia finished in a whisper.

"Will they even realize they're dying?" Wilhelmina inquired.

Navarre shrugged.

"We didn't go into details, 'Mina," he said simply. "Knowing the kind of man Tamaz is, it would be something extremely painful, but fast acting. He would want to kill everyone on *Storm Gauntlet* quickly enough that he could board her, fill Sykora with the antidote, if she wasn't just the carrier vector to begin with, and then steal the ship. He'd have a brand new warship in his fleet, as well as his revenge on everyone. Letting people linger runs the risk that someone cures it, or Sokolov blows the *Gauntlet* in place."

"How long do you suppose, then?" Wilhelmina asked.

Navarre counted the clock in his head.

"Slightly over two hours since exposure," he said. "Piet, how soon until they catch us?"

The navigator tore his eyes away from Navarre and consulted his console.

"We accelerate faster," the man replied finally. "They've got bigger engines so I would guess thirty percent higher top speed in this solar wind density. Maybe four more hours if nothing changes at their end and then…"

Navarre watched him stop talking, his concentration somewhere else. One hand came up to an ear.

Navarre hadn't realized that Piet had an earpiece in, listening to Tamaz on the comm all this time. That took intestinal fortitude, considering the company.

"Sir," Piet said. "You need to hear this."

He reached over and punched a button on the console, dialing up the sound.

A howl of pain filled the cabin.

It was a wail, an angry *ban sidhe* calling for your soul, wordlessly, mindlessly screaming. It took a second for Navarre to realize that a human throat was making it.

Navarre let the chill etch itself into his soul before Javier took over again, relegating the pirate persona back to the dark places inside where a man like that normally resided.

Javier looked individually at his crewmates. Navarre

would have scowled at them. But Navarre was gone. He gave them a hard, purposeful smile instead.

His eyes linked with Wilhelmina. He felt warmth there, but it was across a distant sea, lost across horizons.

"Paladins," he whispered, just loud enough to be heard, "are men and women of the sword."

PART SEVEN

Javier stood to one side of Sokolov's desk and watched the blackness of deep space out a porthole.

Salekhard was gone. Obliterated. Shattered under a rolling salvo of *Storm Gauntlet*'s guns. Purification by immolation. But at that point, it really was just putting down a lame horse. Tamaz and his mad dogs were already dead.

Locals would mark it down to a turf battle between pirates. Those were common enough in places like this. Tamaz had gambled and lost. That was the price you sometimes paid.

"Everyone pays that price eventually, Aritza," the captain replied.

Javier hadn't realized he had spoken aloud in his musings.

"And we might have been able to salvage her," Sokolov continued, almost hopeful.

"No," Javier said firmly. "Better the purging fires. Let hard vac and radiation cleanse the carcass. Anything else risks too much. Who knows what else that bastard had cooked up?"

"So now what, Mister Science Officer?"

"Now?" Javier mused. "We send Sykora and Wilhelmina to complete their mission and sell that ship. Plus we sell the stolen runabout. Then we go on with our lives."

"Are you ever going to tell me the whole story about what happened, Aritza?"

Javier smiled ruefully.

"Not this side of hell, Zakhar. Not this side of hell."

THE BLACK HAIR WAS DISCONCERTING, but she was still beautiful. Javier still saw traces of Hadiiye in the way she moved, but this was Wilhelmina standing before him.

They were alone in his cabin.

He held out a hand, almost shyly.

She took it, almost as carefully.

Silence passed as he sought the words.

"I want you to do something for me," he said finally.

"What?"

"I want to send Suvi with you, 'Mina. She can help protect you out there, and she deserves a chance to escape. I'm going to be stuck a slave for years at this rate. She should live."

"No," Wilhelmina smiled softly at him. She could be a stubborn woman.

"No?"

"No. We talked, her and me."

"You what?"

"Suvi and I talked, while you were with the Captain. I asked her. She wants to stay with you."

Javier turned to face the remote, resting quietly on the charging ring.

"Are you freaking nuts?" he asked.

Suvi's running lights came on.

"You need way more protecting than she does, boss," his first mate, his comrade in surveying, his friend said.

Javier refused to cry as he engulfed Wilhelmina in a hug.

It was good to have friends.

———

JAVIER WATCHED Wilhelmina walk down the airlock tube to the little runabout, just like last time. And just like before, he would never see her again. Although he had made arrangements with her to be at a specific bar on a specific day, five years from now, with a rose in his lapel.

Just in case, you know.

Afia Burakgazi and Piet Alferdinck were already aboard getting ready, like nearly a month hadn't passed since the last time they had tried this. Luck was better the second go round.

He was alone in the airlock.

A tree suddenly appeared behind him, almost silently.

Javier turned.

Djamila Sykora. Dragoon. Ballerina of Death. Angry, angry woman.

She was almost close enough for him to stick his nose into her cleavage. He almost did, anyway.

He looked up.

There was a mad hatred in her eyes.

It was good to be home.

"I've heard most of the story," she growled under her breath.

"Those parts were lies and innuendo," he replied, feeling the heat rise up in his stomach, like bile turned to napalm.

"I have no doubt, Aritza," she snarled. "Especially around you. I want to know why."

"Why what?"

"Why did you agree to it?" she said. "Why risk your life? Why not just walk away? You might like Teague that well, but not Alferdinck or Burakgazi."

"Why did I risk life and limb, freedom and forever, on you, Sykora? Is that it?"

"Exactly, Aritza. Why?"

Javier reached up with his right hand and grabbed her by the shirt front. There was nothing remotely man or woman here, he wanted her down at his level.

He pulled. She came.

They ended up nose to nose, snarl to snarl.

"Because nobody gets to kill you but me," Javier rasped.

Sykora stared hard at him for several seconds, delving as deep into his soul as he went into hers.

He watched the hatred burn in those eyes. That mad, burning rage that overwhelmed every bit of rational thought, of care, of survival. He saw the primal creative energies of the universe. Creation myths unfolding. Pantheonic wars playing out.

Götterdämmerung.

She lunged forward suddenly and kissed him hard on the mouth. It was passion without romance, fire without warmth.

A promise of forever.

Lovers in hatred.

"Deal," she said.

READ MORE!

Be sure to pick up the other books in The Science Officer
series!

The Science Officer
The Mind Field
The Gilded Cage
The Pleasure Dome
The Doomsday Vault
The Last Flagship
The Hammerfield Gambit
The Hammerfield Payoff

You can get volumes 1-4 collected together in
The Science Officer Omnibus 1

Volumes 5-8 are collected together in
The Science Officer Omnibus 2

ABOUT THE AUTHOR

Blaze Ward writes science fiction in the Alexandria Station universe (Jessica Keller, The Science Officer, The Story Road, etc.) as well as several other science fiction universes, such as Star Dragon, the Collective, and more. He also writes odd bits of high fantasy with swords and orcs. In addition, he is the Editor and Publisher of *Boundary Shock Quarterly Magazine*. You can find out more at his website www.blazeward.com, as well as Facebook, Goodreads, and other places.

Blaze's works are available as ebooks, paper, and audio, and can be found at a variety of online vendors (Kobo, Amazon, and others). His newsletter comes out quarterly, and you can also follow his blog on his website. He really enjoys interacting with fans, and looks forward to any and all questions—even ones about his books!

Never miss a release!
If you'd like to be notified of new releases, sign up for my newsletter.

I will never spam you or use your email for nefarious purposes. You can also unsubscribe at any time.

http://www.blazeward.com/newsletter/

Connect with Blaze!

Web: www.blazeward.com
Boundary Shock Quarterly (BSQ):
https://www.boundaryshockquarterly.com/

facebook.com/KRPBlaze
goodreads.com/Blaze_Ward

ABOUT KNOTTED ROAD PRESS

Knotted Road Press fiction specializes in dynamic writing set in mysterious, exotic locations.

Knotted Road Press non-fiction publishes autobiographies, business books, cookbooks, and how-to books with unique voices.

Knotted Road Press creates DRM-free ebooks as well as high-quality print books for readers around the world.

With authors in a variety of genres including literary, poetry, mystery, fantasy, and science fiction, Knotted Road Press has something for everyone.

Knotted Road Press
www.KnottedRoadPress.com